The Return of
Father Brown

The Return of Father Brown

44 NEW MYSTERY STORIES
FEATURING G.K. CHESTERTON'S
INCOMPARABLE PRIEST-DETECTIVE

BY JOHN PETERSON

ACS BOOKS

Cover photo by Dale Ahlquist

Cover and interior design by Ted Schluenderfritz

Cataloging-in-Publication data on file with the Library of Congress.

ISBN 978-0-9744495-1-7

ACS Books is an imprint of TAN Books
PO Box 410487
Charlotte, NC 28241
www.TANBooks.com

Printed and bound in the United States of America.

To
Joan, my wife
and sweetheart

Acknowledgements

The stories in this volume were originally written for *Gilbert Magazine*, the journal of the American Chesterton Society. I am grateful for the support and assistance of this periodical's Editor-in-Chief Sean Dailey, its Literary Editor Therese Warmus, former editors Ronald McCloskey and Eric Scheske, Art Director Theodore Schluenderfritz, and the President of the American Chesterton Society, Dale Ahlquist, who also serves as Publisher of *Gilbert Magazine*.

For further information about the society and its magazine, readers are invited to visit the website:
WWW.CHESTERTON.ORG

Or inquiries may be addressed to:
THE AMERICAN CHESTERTON SOCIETY
4117 PEBBLEBROOK CIRCLE
BLOOMINGTON MN 55437

Table of Contents

Foreword

G. K. CHESTERTON SEEMED TO TAKE GREAT PLEASURE IN diving headlong into the controversies of his time, whether it was art or politics or religion. He could hold his own with writers and thinkers of any ilk, from anarchists to aristocrats, and all the schemers and wire-pullers and reformers and throwbacks in between. But what he really wanted to do was just write detective stories. Unless of course he could just read detective stories. He stated his literary preferences quite clearly: "I would rather have the man who devotes a short story to saying that he can solve the problem of a murder in Margate than the man who devotes a whole book to saying that he cannot solve the problem of things in general."

But Chesterton himself was able to do something few other authors can do, to accomplish those two elusive goals in one story. His character Father Brown not only solves the particular problem of the murder, but also the problem of things in general. And when I say few other authors can achieve this same effect, I mean few. But I know of at least one other besides Chesterton. His name is John Peterson.

When I first got to know John Peterson, I was an aspiring writer, and he was a publisher. He was not just any publisher:

he was my publisher. Over the years, our roles slowly crossed over and switched places. I'm still trying to figure out how that happened, but it is now my happy privilege to publish these stories from his pen.

Back in those glory days of the 1990s, when John was editor of the cleverly-named *Midwest Chesterton News*, he filled space in the most amazing ways. There were plenty of G.K. Chesterton quotations boxed up in a delightful packages, along with many features that would one day become the main pillars in *Gilbert Magazine*. But John began to demonstrate, bit-by-bit, a beyond-deep familiarity with Father Brown. It was a combination of knowing Chesterton, knowing detective fiction, knowing stuff that mere mortals usually do not know. John himself would have made an amusing detective. He has the rigorous logic, the uncanny intuition, the edgy humor, the strange compassion under the gruff exterior, and he has the theology right.

There will never be another Chesterton. But there is still the character of Father Brown, who is simply too fine a fellow to be limited to the 52 stories that Chesterton created for him. He deserves more adventures, and we are grateful that John Peterson has provided those adventures both for him and for us. There is no one on earth more qualified to write *The Return of Father Brown*.

—Dale Ahlquist
President,
American Chesterton Society

Preface

THESE FORTY-FOUR FATHER BROWN STORIES WERE NOT written by G.K. Chesterton, and one cannot but wonder what he would have thought of them. We do have some indication based on his reaction to an article penned in 1923 by the biographer Hesketh Pearson. The item appeared to be a verbatim report of a private quarrel between Chesterton and George Bernard Shaw, and most of those who saw the piece assumed it was authentic. In fact, it was a hoax. There had been no quarrel. Pearson simply invented the entire episode.

Chesterton, delighted with Pearson's audacity, laughingly asked him to ghostwrite his next book for him. Based on that reaction, I do not doubt that, regardless of the merit of these new stories, Chesterton would have taken them as a fine joke, and he would have had a hearty laugh over the very idea.

Sir Arthur Conan Doyle penned just sixty Sherlock Holmes stories; other authors, imitating the Holmes originals, have far exceeded Conan Doyle's own output with an endless stream of new adventures of the great Holmes. By contrast, there have been very few attempts at creating new adventures for other fictional detectives including Father Brown. This is undoubtedly because the reputation of the peerless Holmes towers above that of all other fictional detectives including Father Brown. Furthermore, Conan Doyle's literary style and story formula are, at least in comparison, easier to reproduce; and the mannerisms and speaking style of the eccentric Holmes are instantly recognizable and seemingly tailor-made for imitation and even parody.

None of this is true of Chesterton's stories. Chesterton's witty style is impossible to duplicate, and he deliberately made his priest-detective the opposite of eccentric. As he said in his autobiography, "The point of Father Brown was to appear pointless; and one might say that his conspicuous quality was not being conspicuous."

Unlike his literary rivals, Father Brown had little interest in crime as such. His interest was in sin. After all, he was a priest. The secrets he uncovered were the sins of pride, vindictiveness, and heartlessness from which legal crimes spring, or out of which a mental fog rises up to hide the truth. Other detective-story authors have preferred to employ the concepts of the social sciences when describing the inner lives and motivations of their characters. Chesterton's emphasis on the moral dimension makes Father Brown unique among fictional detectives. Those very few writers who have attempted to write new adventures of Father Brown have chosen not to imitate this emphasis on morality, however; that is surely the main reason these attempts have missed the mark.

The forty-four stories in this book are the result of a request from the editors of *Gilbert Magazine*, the journal of the American Chesterton Society; and to serve the needs of that magazine, they were written in the short-short story format. Thus, they are shorter than the Father Brown originals. Most of these new stories, as most of the original Father Brown stories, involve what critics call "impossible crimes." By this is meant such plot devices as the murder of a victim who was alone in a securely locked room, or the disappearance of a fugitive when every avenue of escape was carefully guarded.

It may be asked why I did not name my priest-detective Father Smith or Father Jones rather than trade on Chesterton's work. It is a fair question—though it never seems to be asked of Conan Doyle's imitators. The easy answer is that it was fun to write stories about Father Brown for the pages of a contemporary magazine dedicated to Chesterton's memory. But these new stories represent also a serious attempt to capture the personality and methods of the original Father Brown as well as to invent new problems of the kind he was so adept at solving.

I enjoyed writing these stories. I sincerely hope they are enjoyable to read. But if all I have accomplished is to send the readers back to Chesterton and his Father Brown, I will rest content.

—John Peterson

Prologue

A CATHOLIC PRIEST KNOWN SIMPLY AS "FATHER BROWN" was, once upon a time, a celebrity in his native England, and his reputation extended even to the United States. Much to his dismay, his genius for helping the police with their most difficult cases gradually found its way into the newspapers. Yet for all his fame, or notoriety, as some called it, he suddenly disappeared from public view. Father Brown made headlines last in 1936 after he exposed an embezzler in one of England's provincial towns.

Some of the priest's many acquaintances supposed that he had retired without fanfare to a monastery. Others thought he might have been given a secret assignment in Rome. There were even a few who feared he might have died among strangers while traveling abroad. More than thirty years were to pass before he once again came to public notice; and, as Father Brown was never one to talk much about himself, his activities during the intervening years remain a mystery to this day.

Father Brown's whereabouts came to light in 1972 when he changed the direction of several criminal investigations in a small town in the American Midwest. Though in his nineties, the priest had lost none of his mental sharpness and was surprisingly vigorous for his age. He had traded his battered black umbrella for a gnarled wooden cane and spent his days serving as a kind of general assistant to the pastor of St. Dominic's, celebrating Mass, instructing catechumens, and spinning tales for the granddaughter of the rectory's housekeeper.

Father Brown would have been quite happy to continue in this anonymous service, and might have done so if his talent for detection had not gradually surfaced and eventually come to the attention of the Bardo County Sheriff's Department. This led to an ever-deepening involvement in the sheriff's business, and it is those stories, in the main, that are reported in the pages that follow.

The Ball and the Cross

FATHER BELL'S FAVORITE CRUCIFIX WAS PLAIN AND UN-adorned, yet it was very beautiful. It had been cast of solid gold and burnished to a high sheen, and though small—it was just under two feet high—it was heavy, and of course quite valuable. It had been hanging in the church to the right of the large statue of Saint Joseph that stood on a pedestal on the side of the altar Catholics used to know as "the epistle side."

Recently one of Father Bell's lay advisors had come to him with a warning about displaying the crucifix. "Times have changed, Father," the man said. "Mark my words, someone is going to come in and carry that cross off and sell it for the value of the gold. Why, it's like hanging a bar of gold bullion on the wall or leaving Krugerrands lying about." When he found that a good number of his other parishioners agreed with this point of view, Father Bell reluctantly gave in and took the crucifix down.

In the symmetrical layout of St. Dominic's church, there is a small room above the sacristy on one side of the altar and a second small room above the vestry on the other side. The room above the sacristy was used as a sort of repository for candelabra, censors, extra chalices—odds and ends—all of which had some value. The room had a sturdy door, which Father Bell kept locked at all times; and he had a locksmith in to change the tumblers so that he could be sure his was the only key that would open it. He had placed the gold crucifix in a large drawer in that room. As he told no one where he had hidden it, he believed he no longer had cause to worry about its safety.

Father Bell also no longer had cause to worry about his new assistant pastor. At first he had doubted that a man in his nineties would be of much help, but he had been pleasantly surprised at the older man's energy and mental agility. Gradually Father Brown had become Father Bell's close friend and wise counselor, and it soon became apparent that many others also valued his counsel. Father Brown often received long distance phone calls, and surprisingly—for this seemed doubly odd to Father Bell—these discussions more often than not appeared to revolve around police business of one kind or another.

"Are you some sort of expert in criminology?" Father Bell had asked.

"Oh, bosh," Father Brown answered with a laugh.

"Well, I've got a crime for you, Father," the younger priest said. He did not seem to be joking.

"Then tell me about it," said Father Brown.

Father Bell began by describing the gold crucifix and ex-plaining his reasons for hiding it in the room above the sacristy. Then he related to Father Brown how he had unlocked the room a few months earlier to find one of the windows broken, glass shards scattered about, and a baseball resting on the floor in a corner. He had swept up the glass and pocketed the ball. He wondered if the guilty lad with the powerful baseball swing would reveal himself in confession, although for some reason that Father Bell could not fathom, young boys seemed to prefer confessing to Father Brown.

"I had an extremely valuable gold crucifix locked up in that room, Father," he continued, "but when I found the smashed window, I did not think to check the drawer where it was hidden. The hole in the window was too small for anyone to enter the room that way. Then, after about a week, I happened to look in the drawer, and discovered that the crucifix was missing.

"According to Sheriff Morley's theory of the crime, the thief probably approached the window on a ladder when no one was there to see him. He knocked a hole in the window, and then he pulled the drawer open and grasped the crucifix with some sort of grappling device on a pole. Sheriff Morley also said that a clever thief would leave the baseball behind as a ruse—to explain the broken window."

The story made Father Brown smile.

"So tell me," Father Bell asked, "is this the sort of puzzle you might be able to work out, Father Brown?"

Father Brown shook his head. "If the thief were a professional," he said, "there would be very little chance of tracing him."

"And if the thief is an amateur?"

Father Brown paused for a moment, and seemed to be gathering his thoughts—or perhaps choosing his words. "Well," he said at last, "when an ordinary sort of person happens upon something of great value, he might be tempted to bear it off; but he probably will not see the problems involved or think through his plan. In the end, he will often be stumped by the realization that he can't sell the thing—or indeed even return it—without being exposed as a thief. If his conscience won't let him simply discard it, then, often, a kind of paralysis sets in while he waits for an opportunity or an idea."

"And you're convinced this theft was the work of an amateur?"

"I am inclined to think so," said Father Brown. "But let me mull this over for a while."

Later in the day, when Father Bell was puttering about in the vestry, Father Brown appeared in the doorway with a package tucked under his arm.

"Have you a moment, Father?" the older priest asked.

"Why, of course," said Father Bell.

"Then please unwrap this parcel and let me have your opinion of its contents."

"It's heavy for its size," Father Bell said. He put the package on a counter and loosened the string. Then he could only gasp in surprise and joy as he gazed down at the gold crucifix. "How... how...how...?" he stuttered.

"We magicians never reveal our secrets," Father Brown said with a chuckle. "Still, I can tell you that the thief, whose name I must not tell you, is now penitent, has made restitution, and has been granted amnesty."

"I still can't believe it," Father Bell said, shaking his head in wonder. "Thanks," he said grasping the old priest's hand, "just plain *thanks*."

"My dear fellow," said Father Brown.

"There's just one thing I'd like to know, and that's how the theft was done. I wouldn't ask if the answer would reveal who the thief was, but if he described the sort of apparatus he used to fish the cross out of that drawer—well, I can't imagine what it would look like. I'm just curious."

"I'm sorry," Father Brown said with all due gravity. "We did not discuss what you and I refer to as 'method' and the police refer to as 'means.'"

"Well, anyhow, I'm taking this crucifix right now and hanging it back up in the church where it belongs—for better or for worse."

"Good," said Father Brown, and then he walked out of the vestry leaning heavily on his knobby cane. As he plodded down the side aisle of the church, he noticed Silas the custodian kneeling in a pew and praying. Silas looked up and gave Father Brown a barely perceptible nod, which the priest returned with a nod that was little more than a lowering of his eyelids.

Perhaps he is reciting his penance, Father Brown thought to himself, or whispering a prayer of thanksgiving. Custodians, of course, can be relied upon to repair any windows that happen to get themselves broken by baseballs. Left alone to work, a custodian might also have a lively curiosity about what is hidden in the drawers of a room that has always been kept carefully locked.

Such a man would surely have every reason to be thankful for the forgiveness of God. And for priests like Father Brown.

The Safe

JOEL LOVED HIS TALKS WITH THE LITTLE PRIEST FROM England. Father Brown, though now in his nineties, was still witty and more important yet, a good listener. Joel, a talkative man now in his seventies, found good listeners hard to find. Still, he noticed that the priest was more interested than usual when the subject turned to a recent burglary. The heightened interest echoed Father Brown's former avocation as an amateur sleuth.

Joel's story began in the previous year when his friend Potts canceled his safety deposit box at the bank and, as a matter of economy and convenience, purchased a small fireproof safe for his valuables. He had placed the safe on a counter in a store-room—a room he always kept locked. It was an interior room without windows and lined with drawers, shelves, and cabinets.

Joel had thought these arrangements rather futile. "A thief could break into that room and then carry the safe away," he said with a harsh laugh. "He'd worry at his leisure about getting the safe open."

"How would a thief know I have a safe?" Potts had replied.

"How should I know?" Joel said. "He might just be looking for any sort of valuables he could find."

Potts was not convinced.

To Joel's surprise, when the theft occurred Potts found the storeroom door not forced but rather unlocked. The safe stood in its accustomed place on the counter, its door standing open.

"Potts swears he gave the combination to no one," Joel explained to Father Brown, "but young Tim was convinced his dad had chosen an easy-to-guess number—his birth date perhaps, or zip code."

"Tim lives with him?" Father Brown asked.

"No," Joel replied, "he's vacationing from college at present." Then he added, "Some might say he is also on vacation when *at* college. The lad is something of a ne'er-do-well."

"Does Tim have the use of his father's motor car when he visits?"

"Yes, of course," Joel said. "He gave me a lift just the other day. Why do you ask, Father Brown?"

"Just a fancy of mine," said the priest. "Pray continue."

Joel explained that the value of the contents of the safe had been substantial. There were negotiable bearer bonds worth almost twenty thousand dollars and some one-ounce gold coins that anyone could trade in for cash.

"About that combination to the safe," Father Brown asked, "was it one that might be easily guessed?"

"No one could have guessed it," Joel answered. "It was '80-10-10,' a metallurgist's common recipe for brass, followed by '54-40,' from an old dispute about the Oregon Territory boundary."

"Fifty-four forty or fight!" said the priest. "Oh, don't look surprised, Joel. Of course I know that old slogan—my own country was involved in the dispute. Potts trusted *you* with the combination, then?"

"Oh, no," Joel said. "He was reluctant to tell us even after the theft, but his son pointed out that it was a bit late in the game for that sort of caution. I think Potts told us the combination just to show his son he wasn't the sort of fool who would use an easily guessable number. After his wife ran away, Potts had to be both mother and father to the lad; and I suspect the son's wildness is a way of striking back at the absent mother. But really, Potts has badly spoiled Tim."

"How did Potts acquire his safe?" the priest asked.

"Oh, it was a standard model," Joel said. "Bought it from one of those big office supply emporiums, I believe. Anyway, Sheriff Morley has no leads, and the reluctant insurance company is saying they have no proof that a theft actually occurred."

■   ■   ■

A week later, a somewhat puzzled Joel gave the priest the latest news on the burglary. "Potts has withdrawn his insurance claim. The police have dropped the case. No one will even discuss it with me."

"Then let *us* not discuss it," said Father Brown.

"Well, I'm getting to the bottom of it," Joel said sternly, "if it kills me."

The priest regarded him for a long minute. Then he sighed and said, "You are a friend of the Potts family. Believe me, Joel, it is best for them if we forget this foolish episode. I will tell you about it, but only if I have your word that you will not discuss it with any living soul, and especially not with Mr. Potts."

"All right," Joel said after a moment.

"From what you told me," the priest began, "the entire business came down to a matter of family faithfulness. And that's why it was more than criminal that young Tim should steal from his father."

"It was Tim?"

"Of course it was Tim," said the priest. "Who *else* would it be? Who else *could* it be? I had a long talk with the youngster, and he began to see that if his father somehow uncovered what he had done, it would strike a heartfelt blow to the poor gentleman. Then the two of us went together, and Tim told his father the truth. In the aftermath, I rather think they now have a more wholesome father and son friendship. I fear that relations between them had become dangerously childish. Oh, and of course we settled things with the police. Our pastor, Father Bell, has some good friends in city government.

"But you're wondering about the method. People always fasten on the silly mechanics of a crime. Well, it was obvious—or at least it was to me—that Tim had simply bought a duplicate safe. That wasn't his father's safe, it was Tim's own safe on the counter with its door hanging open. Then he wheedled the combination to the other safe out of his father, took the valuables, and switched safes one final time. It was all quite obvious from what you told me."

"But how did he get into the locked room?"

"My dear Joel," Father Brown said, "if Potts trusted his son with his car, he must have trusted him with his keys. It is not difficult getting duplicates made, or so I've been led to understand."

"So, Father," Joel said, "I guess to your way of thinking, the real crime was Tim's abuse of the privilege of using his father's car and his keys."

"Well, as to that," said Father Brown, "it was not so much the abuse of his father's kindnesses that troubled me. It was the abuse of his father's trust."

The Locked Room

I CAME TO SEE YOU," BERT SAID, "BECAUSE I'VE HEARD IT rumored that you're an expert on locked-room murders."

"Yes, I suppose I am," the old priest replied, and regarded his energetic young friend with a broad smile. "For more years than I can remember, I made myself a nuisance to the police over every sort of crime. But in all those years I never once saw a murder committed in a locked room. I never expect to see one. If that qualifies me as an expert on the subject, I'm at your service."

"Well, this was a murder in a locked room," Bert said. "Nobody disputes that. The victim was locked in and the murderer, whoever he was, was locked out."

"Well, tell me all about it then," said Father Brown.

"I've already told you about Fair Lane Arts, Father, the teachers' college where I work as a language instructor. It's a small, one-building affair, three stories and a parking lot." The priest nodded.

"It was Sunday afternoon and only five of us were working there. I was in a classroom when I heard a man's loud agonized scream. I ran to the file room next door where I thought the scream came from. The door has a wood frame enclosing a large glass panel, like most classroom doors; and there at the end of the aisle between filing cabinets, I could see our math teacher, Nelson, slumped in a chair with a large red bloodstain on his white shirtfront and a pretty wicked-looking knife on the floor in front of him."

"The door was locked?" asked the priest.

"Yes, it was definitely locked, and I could see the key sticking out of the keyhole on the other side of the door. By this time Lois, the librarian, had run up, out of breath. She wanted to break the glass, but I knew the thick safety glass wouldn't break easily. I went to find the custodian, and Lois went to phone for an ambulance. When we came back, Heller, the physics and chemistry instructor, was kneeling in front of the door trying to dislodge the key by shoving a rod into the keyhole."

"You say no one else was there in the school?" the priest asked.

"No, just the four of us and poor Nelson," Noel said. "At least, we were the only ones who signed in at the front door. But I suppose somebody else could have come in without signing the sheet."

"Were you all friends as well as colleagues?"

"Not in the slightest, except for Nelson and Heller. They were collaborating on an important discovery in some arcane area of applied mathematics. They were preparing a paper they thought would make them famous."

"How did you get into the room?" asked Father Brown.

"Very deftly," Bert said. He then described how Heller had taken charge and how he had slid a newspaper page under the door. When he dislodged the key with the rod, according to Bert's account, it fell onto the paper. Heller was then able to pull it back out, and he used the key to unlock the door.

"Heller asked if any of us had any medical training," Bert continued, "Peters, the custodian, said he had been a corpsman, so Heller told him to see to Nelson and give him first aid. But, he said, if Peters found the man was dead, then he should leave everything just as it was and come back out of the room. Peters did find Nelson dead, as it turned out; so, we waited there in the doorway for the sheriff and his men, who after a very thorough search found no murderer hiding in the room.

"There are no windows or other doors or large air vents in the file room, Father, if you're thinking about possible ways the murderer might have escaped. Sheriff Morley said it was not suicide, and he ruled out any kind of device that could fling a knife by remote control. He is baffled."

"Will Heller finish the mathematical discovery and publish it on behalf of his friend?"

"Actually, no," Bert said. "Heller says the ideas were mostly his, Father, and the prestige won't do Nelson any good now that he's gone."

"I see," said the priest. "So that's how it was."

Bert's eyebrows arched in surprise. "So you've solved a locked room mystery after all," he said, excitedly. "Will you tell me how it happened?"

"Will you promise not to repeat it?" said Father Brown. "I want to have a chat with the guilty party, you know, about contrition and...and other things."

"You have my word, Father. I'll say nothing to anyone."

"It's a sad business," said the old priest. "Partners so easily become rivals, and rivals so easily become enemies. I believe the two men quarreled over how the credit for their great discovery should be divided between them, and both men wanted the superior role. The dispute was settled with bloodshed, exactly as a similar dispute was settled between Cain and Abel so long ago."

"But how..."

"I don't know how much of Heller's performance was planned," said Father Brown, "or how much was improvisation.

I expect he thought to hide behind a filing cabinet; and then when you broke into the room and rushed to the victim, he would simply have stepped out behind you and become the last member of your group. But when he saw that you and Lois had left the door unguarded, he unlocked it; and leaving the key in the keyhole inside, he stepped out. Next, he placed the newspaper under the door, and then he pretended the door was still locked and began fiddling with that rod."

"Why, the way you explain it," Bert said, "it sounds so obvious. But you were wrong about one thing, at least, Father Brown."

"I often am," said the priest, "but what was my mistake this time?"

"You said murders don't happen in locked rooms. This one did."

"Well, then," said Father Brown with a hearty laugh, "let us celebrate my error. I know where there's a bottle of very good claret, and here at St. Dominic's, thank heaven, such things are never kept in locked rooms."

The Relic

TWO LAW ENFORCEMENT OFFICIALS AND TWO PRIESTS sat down at a table in the rectory of St. Dominic's church. The officials were a lumpy middle-aged man named Morley, who was the county sheriff, and a steely-eyed younger man named Sloan, who was an FBI investigator. The priests were Father Bell, the pastor, and his assistant, who seemed remarkably spry for a man in his nineties. His name was Brown.

Before the four men could begin their discussion, a young lady of about five or six years toddled into the room bearing a large book. She walked straight up to the chair in which the old priest was sitting and clambered up onto his lap. Sheriff Morley gestured impatiently. "Can we get on with this?" he said. "My time is valuable."

The priest and the child discussed the situation briefly, if somewhat noisily, and then the girl dutifully slid from his lap and walked off with her book. "I beg your pardon," the priest said. "Lizzie is our housekeeper's granddaughter. She and I are halfway through a profound study of the life and times of Br'er Rabbit."

"Can we get serious?" Morley asked.

The old priest took a moment to gather his thoughts about the events of the last two days. On Wednesday afternoon, a priceless relic had been stolen from the church. The reliquary in which it had been displayed was a heavy glass case, padded on the bottom so that when it was moved there would be no unseemly clinking or scraping. Of course, the case was kept securely locked so that its contents could be viewed but not handled. Yet by afternoon's end, a worthless copy was discovered to have replaced the true relic.

The missing item was believed on good if not absolute authority to have been the personal rosary of St. Dominic, and an unfounded but widely circulated rumor said it had been fashioned in heaven and given to Dominic by the Virgin Mary. The large and beautifully wrought rosary was traveling from cathedral to cathedral throughout North America, and crowds of pious pilgrims and curious tourists lined up at each stop to view it.

The theft occurred in one of the very few stops that was not a cathedral. The privilege had been granted partly because the church was dedicated to St. Dominic and partly because, as Pastor Bell explained, "The bishop *owed* me one."

The case or reliquary that held the rosary had been placed on a pedestal at the front of the church's center aisle, and a uniformed guard was stationed directly behind it. Father Bell replaced this man for an hour at lunchtime and for three or four short intervals during which, as the pastor reported, "the man overwhelmed the outdoor Marian grotto with cigarette smoke."

Many of St. Dominic's parishioners had been waiting for the formal devotional service scheduled for that evening; and, as this was a small parish in a small town, the lines throughout the day had not been very long. Viewing proceeded without incident except for one strange interlude when a young woman rushed out of the sacristy, murmuring that she would touch the rosary of St. Dominic "or die in the attempt." A priest had pursued her, and he managed to persuade her to leave. Thus far, the sheriff's police had not located either the priest or the woman for questioning.

According to the guard, the priest had restrained this woman before she came within thirty feet of the pedestal, and the entire incident had taken no more than about ten or fifteen seconds. Silas, the parish custodian, was on the scene because he had kindly volunteered to help a wheelchair-bound visitor. His testimony backed up the guard precisely. No one else could be found who was in the church at the time; but the testimony of the guard and the custodian could not reasonably be doubted, for the two men were strangers to each other and there was no connection of any kind between them.

Sheriff Morley jolted Father Brown back to the present. "Hey!" he said, perhaps more harshly than strict etiquette would allow. "Do you have something to tell us or not?"

"I will say this," the priest replied. "Holy relics seem to attract some combination of pilgrims, tourists, fanatics, and thieves. It has always been so. I have spent the better part of this afternoon in conversation with two fanatics who are, in this case, also thieves. I have persuaded them to give up the precious rosary—"

"You what?" said Agent Sloan.

"—but there are terms," said Father Brown.

"Terms?" asked Sheriff Morley. "What terms?"

"If the culprits," said Father Brown, "are not identified, arrested, harassed, pursued, or exposed in any way, the rosary will be returned immediately and undamaged. That is the bargain I made with them in order to secure the rosary's safe return."

"It's the sheriff's jurisdiction," Sloan said, "but I've been told that recovering the relic is the first consideration."

"Do I have your word that the authorities will not harass the thieves?"

"If you have the relic," Sloan replied.

"Sheriff?" said Father Brown, turning in his seat to face Morley.

"Yes, I agree," said Morley, "but I don't for a second believe you can deliver on your promise, Parson."

"I also spent some time with Silas, our custodian," said Father Brown. "He was paid for what he did, but he is properly ashamed of himself now. That woman and her companion in priest's costume caused a fuss to draw the guard's attention. He was watching them intently when Silas exchanged the glass case on the pedestal for a duplicate the man in the wheelchair had hidden under his lap blanket. It was obvious from the first that the fanatical woman's purpose was designed as a diversion, and the rest of the scheme was easy enough to work out."

"I don't buy it," Morley said. "A guard would have seen the switch out of the corner of his eye. He would have been aware of movement of some sort, and he'd have glanced back."

"Would *you* have glanced back?" Father Brown asked. "*Did* you glance back?" Then he pointed to the table where—not five feet from Morley's left elbow—they saw a heavy glass case with a rosary resting inside. "That's the original case and the true relic," Father Brown said. "Our good pastor put it on the table while you were watching Lizzie climb onto my lap. I must say, she played her part to perfection."

"A cheap trick," said Morley.

"On the contrary," said Father Bell, "a valuable demonstration."

"I think Lizzie may still have time for a chapter of *Uncle Remus*," said Father Brown. "Her time really *is* valuable. Good night, gentlemen."

Doctor Fern's Clinic

FATHER BROWN COULD ALMOST ALWAYS BE FOUND SOME-where at St. Dominic's—if not in the church then in the parish rectory. He hobbled about these premises energetically with the help of his knobby cane, looking for ways to be helpful or simply for ways to be friendly.

The old priest would not have become involved in the most recent criminal case in Bardo County if he had not followed his Master's command to visit those in prison or, in this case, the county jail. A local man named Donald Croft had been arrested and was being held there without bail.

Croft was an active member of the Evangelical Free Church and one of the mainstays of the county's Pro-Life League. He was a large-boned and burley man who could be a daunting presence when he was picketing at the newly established local abortion clinic. He was sometimes the lone protester—carrying a sign, handing out literature, and attempting to engage the clinic's customers in friendly but purposeful conversation.

When the clinic was firebombed, the owner, a small, nervous doctor named Fern, was very nearly trapped inside. The newspapers reported that Fern had been near the front door when the explosion occurred, and he had been able to escape without injury. He had also been able to accost Mr. Croft as the latter exited the building though a side door. The men grappled, but after a short struggle, Croft, much the stronger of the two, broke free. Doctor Fern then asked a neighboring businessman—who had come on the run when he heard the explosion—to summon the fire brigade and the sheriff's police.

A forensic examination of Croft's clothing revealed minute particles of ammonium nitrate and fuel oil, the ingredients used in the homemade bomb that destroyed the abortuary. Croft was summarily charged with arson and attempted murder, and his conviction appeared all but certain.

"Is there anything we might do for you?" Father Brown asked.

"Or is there something for our parishioners to do?" Father Bell asked.

The three men were seated at a table in a secure room inside the jail under the watchful eyes of one of the sheriff's deputies.

"Thank you," Croft said. "I have had wonderful support from my own congregation. They believe my side of the story."

"I don't believe we know your side of the story," Father Brown replied. "The newspapers have not been very helpful in that regard. Pray tell us what happened."

"It was my bad luck that the explosion went off when I was picketing all by myself," Croft said, "and so I have no friendly witnesses. But anyway I knew Doctor Fern was inside the clinic, and I went in to see if I could help him. As it was, I couldn't stay in that inferno for more than a second. The heat was unbearable. When I came out, it seemed to me that Fern was looking for me. When he saw me, he jumped me and we tumbled to the ground together. He was cursing me and accusing me of bombing his clinic. Well, I had no trouble brushing him off. I didn't hurt him."

"You didn't set off that explosion?" Father Bell asked.

"No, I didn't," Croft answered calmly. "And there really wasn't any reason to. Our sidewalk counseling has been such a success that the abortion clinic was going broke. Fern was going to have to close it down."

"You explained all this to the sheriff?" Father Brown asked.

"Of course."

Father Brown seemed lost in his thoughts for a moment. At last, he sighed and said, "Well, I'm at a loss to explain how he missed the obvious."

As the two priests left the jail, Father Brown mentally sorted through his possible avenues of approach. After due reflection, he made several long-distance phone calls. There was nothing more he could do then but to wait and to pray.

After three weeks had passed, Father Brown phoned Sheriff Morley and asked him to visit the rectory. When Morley showed some resistance to the invitation, Father Brown assured him that he had something of importance to say about the clinic bombing. The sheriff agreed but with a greater reluctance than seemed reasonable, or so it appeared to the priest.

"Make it quick, Parson," Morley said, after Mrs. James had shown him into the parlor. "I don't have time for sermons from anti-abortion fanatics."

"I thought it would be unfair to you, Sheriff," Father Brown said, "if I did not warn you that there is new evidence."

"And how could someone like you possibly know that?" Morley asked.

Father Brown seemed amused by the question. "Well," he said with a laugh, "surprisingly enough, I have some friends. One of them kindly pursued an idea or two I had about the case. I just heard from him—a man named Cummings. He's with the Chicago office of your Federal Bureau of Investigation. He has done some digging for us, and he's discovered thatDoctor Fern purchased a quantity of ammonium nitrate a few months back." The sheriff's eyebrows lifted, but he said nothing.

"There are other facts," Father Brown continued. "For one thing, Doctor Fern's abortion business was failing, and my own inquiries have informed me that he has been trying to sell the clinic, though without success. Agent Cummings found out that the abortuary was heavily insured against damage by fire. And last, I think a moment's reflection on that foolish wrestling bout immediately after the explosion will explain how the damning residue evidence was transferred from Doctor Fern to Mr. Croft."

The sheriff did not seem pleased by these revelations. "Why you meddling old fool," he said, and with no further ceremony he marched through the door and was gone.

Oh dear, Father Brown said to himself, obviously Sheriff Morley does not welcome the truth—still, with Agent Cummings looking over his shoulder, he will have no choice but to do the right thing.

"Well, 'to dinner come,'" he said aloud in the empty room, quoting his favorite poet, "'I hope we shall drink down all unkindness.'"

He had no inkling then that his meddling in the Croft affair would lead to an ever-deepening involvement in the business of the sheriff's department.

The Shoe

I T WAS A CHILLY AUTUMN DAY AS LILLY CARR PICKED UP the last bit of litter from the roadside at the rear of her property. She was a fussy old widow, some thought, with a ridiculous passion or phobia about litter. As she saw it, she was being of service to the community. Lilly turned to survey her work and, to her dismay, she saw one more bit of junk lying on the grassy shoulder of the road that she thought she had picked clean. The litterbugs can't even wait until I finish, she thought with a flash of anger.

She stooped to pick up the shoe—a man's black sneaker and a fairly new one. Lilly was surprised that the inside of the shoe was warm and moist to the touch. Isn't that odd, Lilly thought. She hadn't noticed any joggers.

She looked up and down the road, but the only car she saw was the sheriff's familiar Ford sedan. It was coming toward her and heading for the center of the small town. She waved to Sheriff Morley, but he kept his eyes on the road as he drove past her. She did not like Sheriff Morley.

Lilly took the bags of litter out to the street in front of her house. The trash collectors were due later that morning, but she didn't throw the shoe away. Instead, she phoned Ray's

Department Store. Then she called her friend Marie Dirks, whose husband, at least in Ray's opinion, was the owner of the black shoe.

◾   ◾   ◾

Lilly was delighted when Father Brown rang her doorbell later that morning. He was a very old but still vigorous Roman priest, from England originally. He had come for morning tea because, as he said, Lilly brewed the only decent tea west of the Hebrides. Lilly was happy to have his pleasant company.

She told Father Brown all about the shoe. "Marie was happy I found it," Lilly said, "but she couldn't imagine how it landed at my back door. She phoned again to say she called her husband— he's a deputy sheriff—and was told they didn't know where he was. That was odd. But it's just another of this morning's peculiar events."

"What else has happened?" the priest asked.

"The sheriff came by to see my water bill for last month. That in itself seemed peculiar. He said he was making a random check for errors. The strange thing was, when I came back into this room, he had closed the drapes at the picture window. I like the drapes open. It was as though he didn't want passersby to see him in my house."

"That's one interpretation," said the priest.

"A little while later," Lilly said, "I saw the trash collector's truck rumble by without stopping. I rushed out to try to flag them down, but then I saw that my trash was gone. Somehow, they must have managed to pick it up on the run. It was just one more puzzle in a very puzzling morning—is something wrong, Father Brown?"

"Do you keep a loaded gun in the house?" Father Brown asked. "I'm afraid there is just one way of reading the curious events you've described. It makes an ugly story."

Less than an hour had passed when Sheriff Morley walked through the front door of St. Dominic's parish rectory and confronted the two priests who resided there. "Reverend," he said to Father Brown, "I want to have a private word with Lilly Carr. I know she's here." Instead of answering, Father Brown held out the black sneaker. It was strangely discolored and torn.

"If you're wondering, Sheriff," he said, "those are bullet holes. I had Mrs. Carr shoot it with her husband's rifle."

"Obstruction of justice," the sheriff said.

"No," said Father Bell, "it isn't obstructing anything, Sheriff. It was done in the service of justice. Its purpose is to slow you down and make you think."

"Your car was following deputy Dirks' car," Father Brown said without further preliminaries. "You were heading out of town and probably on your way to a fatal 'accident'. Dirks must have been tied up or held down. Somehow he managed to push the door open and flip his left shoe off so that it dropped by the side of the road. You didn't want to have to explain how an accident victim came to be missing a shoe, so you turned your car around. But there was Lilly picking up litter."

"You have quite an imagination," the sheriff said.

"You saw the trash bags sitting at the curb in front of Lilly's house, and you thought she might have put the shoe in one of them along with the rest of the litter she had collected. But you couldn't have someone put the bags in your car with her watching through her big window—you know very little escapes her notice—so you came in and closed the drapes. Of course, you didn't find the shoe in the trash bags. And next, Lilly saw the refuse truck pass by without stopping."

Then, seeming to change the subject, Father Brown asked, "How does an accident victim come to be wearing a shoe riddled with bullet holes? I suppose you may not need to answer that question. You'll be in charge of the investigation. How smoothly things must work when you're a criminal and everyone accepts you as their sheriff. Except for poor Dirks, of course; he found you out."

Morley took a step toward the priest, but the little man continued in a calm voice. "Father Bell and I have had a long telephone discussion with that old friend of mine named Cummings. And he left a message for you." Father Brown inclined his head toward the answering machine on the table.

Without another word, Sheriff Morley walked over to the machine and pressed a button. "You have one message," the mechanical voice said; and then a new voice began speaking:

"Sheriff Morley, this is Agent Cummings of the FBI in Chicago. I've just finished deposing Lilly Carr by telephone. Your state police are notified. You don't have much time, Morley, but this message is to warn you not to harm Mrs. Carr or the priests. If Deputy Dirks is still alive, let him go, unless you want a murder rap on top of everything else. Goodbye."

Morley stared at the phone for ten seconds. Then he wheeled around and almost ran out of the rectory. Father Brown never saw the man again, but later he was pleased to be introduced to Acting Sheriff Dirks, who, the priest could not fail to notice, was alive and well. Dirks wore a broad grin.

"I'll never know how to thank you," he said to Father Brown.

"Well, there's something I do each morning," the priest replied. "I thank God for Mrs. Carr's tea. And we mustn't forget, Mr. Dirks, it was her hospitality to me that saved your life."

The Exact Time

FATHER BROWN DID NOT OWN A WATCH AND HE NEVER used an alarm clock. He simply woke up at about five in the morning each day as a matter of long habit. The day of the murder was no exception.

After dressing, he climbed down the stairs of the rectory and, leaning a bit on his knobby cane, he trudged the few steps to the church next door. He liked to begin his day by kneeling in the sanctuary and praying before the tabernacle. After taking out a key to unlock the front door of the church, the old priest heard something that made him pause.

Father Brown was getting a bit deaf, but he was quite sure he had just heard a gunshot. Then there was, it seemed to him, a prolonged shout or moan somewhere in the distance. He turned around but he could not see much in the darkness. The lighted clock-face in the tower of the First National Bank building stood out starkly in the gloom, and he saw that it was exactly twenty-five minutes after five. Father Brown entered the church and closed the door behind him.

It wasn't until the day dawned that the crumpled body of the bank's president, Jay Wood, was found at the base of the clock tower, a bullet wound in his back. The medical examiner's preliminary finding was that the man had been standing in the roofed pavilion above the clock when he was shot, and that he had then stumbled over the parapet to his death. It was the fall that had killed him. The estimated time of death was sometime between between five and five-thirty in the morning.

Sheriff Dirks was a tall and slender man—so tall that when he questioned witnesses he had learned not to tower over them, for that could be intimidating. His shaggy and graying mustache softened his sharp features and gave him a kindly look. Dirks had become exceptionally adept at gathering facts; although, in truth, his deputies were not as confident about his ability to put the facts together and make them add up.

He had quickly learned from the cleaning crew and custodian that it was not unusual for banker Wood, a workaholic, to be on the job before sunup. Shortly before five that morning, they all agreed, Wood had received a visitor, but they had not seen who it was. Wood must have wanted privacy, the one reason they could imagine that would send him and another person up to the pavilion to avoid being overheard. None of these witnesses had heard the gunshot.

Dirks was almost certain he knew the identity of the killer. Banker Wood had been a divorced man with a grudge, and he had made it his life's ambition to ruin a man named Paxton, who had stolen his wife and destroyed his marriage. Bankers can often pull strings in the financial whirl of a small town, and it was widely believed that for revenge Wood was maneuvering Paxton in the direction of bankruptcy. If Wood was murdered then Paxton was his murderer. Still, a sheriff has to avoid careless accusations.

As he left the bank, Dirks glanced at the tower and saw that the time displayed by the big clock agreed with his wristwatch, as it always did. It was nine-thirty. By noon, and to his displeasure, he had established that Paxton had a good if not exactly a perfect alibi. Six people were willing to swear that Paxton had walked into Mary's Coffee Shop at precisely five-twenty that morning. It meant that Dirks would have to be much more precise about the time of the murder.

That night during the supper hour, the sheriff spoke into the microphone of Bardo County's only radio station to make a heartfelt appeal to anyone who might have heard or seen anything suspicious in the vicinity of the First National Bank between five and six that morning. "Please, please help us," he said, and Father Brown phoned almost immediately. Dirks was not a profane man, but as he cradled the phone, he cursed freely. According to what the priest said about the time of the gunshot, Paxton had been sitting in Mary's Coffee Shop when Wood the banker fell from his tower.

It was in the evening a week later that the sheriff paid a call at the rectory of St. Dominic's. He found Father Brown immersed in conversation with Hal Lund, a custodian who worked at the First National Bank. Lund was a regular visitor at the rectory because Father Brown was the only one in the small town who had sufficient knowledge and patience for Hal's long discussions about the adventures and investigations of Sherlock Holmes.

"Father," Sheriff Dirks said, "we've had to drop our investigation of Bart Paxton."

"I know," said Father Brown. "He came to see me this afternoon. He told me he wanted to thank me for my testimony. Still, I couldn't help but think he came less in gratitude and more in an attempt to gauge how confident I was of my facts."

"Seems to me that's what a guilty man would do," Dirks said.

"That thought had crossed my mind," agreed Father Brown.

"What did you tell him?"

"I told him he should return to the Church and her sacraments."

"And what did he say to that?" the sheriff asked.

"He said he no longer had time for that sort of nonsense."

"Well, Father Brown," Dirks said, "I have to ask you just once more. Are you still certain of the time?"

"I'm sorry, Sheriff," said the priest. "It was dark, and that lighted clock on the tower stood out like a beacon. I can still picture it."

At that moment, Hal jumped to his feet. "The...the clock?" he stammered. Then before Father Brown could answer him, he spoke on in rising excitement. "I didn't realize the clock on the tower had anything to do with this! Listen, at a quarter-to-six that morning, I was on the job at the bank, and Mrs. Larue came 'round and said that the clock was fifteen minutes fast. And I said I have never known it to be wrong by so much as a minute, but I popped upstairs for a look. She was right, and so I set it back."

"Why the hell didn't you come forward with this?" said the sheriff with some heat.

"I had no idea it meant anything," Hal said.

Father Brown held up his hands. "Just give me space to think," he said, brushing one hand through his stubby white hair. After a moment's silence he said, "Is it possible that when poor Mr. Wood fell from that pavilion, he reached out in desperation and clutched at the minute hand as he fell? Could the weight of his body have pulled the hand down a distance of fifteen minutes before he let it go? If it did, it means I heard that gunshot at ten minutes after five."

Dirks was already heading out of the room with a very grim smile on his face.

"Now, perhaps," Father Brown said, to himself it seemed, "Mr. Paxton may once again find the time for my sort of nonsense."

The Man Who Knew Too Much

IT WAS A COLD AND GRAY NOVEMBER DAY IN LONDON, BUT the Duke of Tsergovia smiled warmly at his loyal head of security. Then he shook his head. "This I must do myself, Rudolf," he said. "I will be safe enough. The suitcase will confuse the police. It is what the British call a red herring." Both men chuckled at this. "And if the red herring is not sufficiently confusing, I have an insurance policy, eh?"

"You have designed the perfect murder, Excellency," said the other man. "The satisfaction and pleasure of pulling the trigger should be yours."

It was three full years after this conversation that Inspector Greenwood, now retired and traveling on holiday in the States, was pleased to locate his old friend Father Brown and to renew their friendship. The priest was delighted to see him after the space of so many years, and they both enjoyed reminiscing about the murders and thefts of those bygone days. Finally, Greenwood opened a subject he hoped Father Brown would find even more interesting.

"It was three years ago," Greenwood said. "Do you recall some rather lurid headlines along the lines of 'Dwarf-Sized Killer Hides in Suitcase'?"

"It seems an idea fit for a detective story," said Father Brown.

"It was no fiction, I assure you." And so the inspector told his old friend how a London gossip columnist named Olsen had been shot to death in his own office in the middle of the afternoon. No weapon had been found, and it was all but certain the killer had used a gun with a silencer, for no one, not even Olsen's secretary, had heard the shots. The police were also quite sure the culprit left the third-floor office by means of a rope ladder, which they had found attached to an open window.

"Here's the part that was sensationalized by the newspapers," Greenwood said. "The killer appeared to have been smuggled into the office inside of a suitcase that was tricked out with breathing tubes and peep holes. A microscopic examination of residue found in the suitcase showed that some person must have stayed inside it for a considerable length of time—perhaps as long as several hours. It was a very small suitcase, and anyone hiding in it could not have been taller than four feet, three inches."

"Thus those headlines about a dwarf-sized killer," said Father Brown.

"The local community of little people was horrified by the publicity, of course," Greenwood said, "and they tried to help us. But we could not find the slightest connection between any of them and Olsen."

"And who was Olsen's last visitor before the murder?"

"I can tell you in confidence," Greenwood said, "that the last visitor was the Duke of Tsergovia. Yes, he was carrying a suitcase, presumably because he was on his way to Heathrow to catch a flight. Anyhow, his suitcase was of an entirely different color and style from the one left in the office; and Olsen's secretary says she could tell by the way he carried it that it did not harbor anything so heavy as a human being, even a very small one. And we know the duke took his suitcase with him when he left."

"Do you know what he did with it?" Father Brown asked.

"In that regard, we were remarkably lucky. Olsen had one of his stringers following the duke, and he saw the man jump into a taxi. The stringer followed it to the airport and watched the duke walk directly to his gate and board a plane for New York. At no time did he set his suitcase down, except when (as the taxi driver later told us) he took off his raincoat and gloves and packed them in the suitcase during the ride to the airport."

"Did the duke know he was being followed?" asked the priest.

"Almost certainly he did," said Greenwood, "but that doesn't change the facts." The inspector went on to say that New Scotland Yard had asked the FBI to question the duke on his arrival in New York. They were thorough in metal-scanning everyone who left the plane as well as all of their carry-on luggage and parcels. The duke was surprisingly cooperative. He insisted they search him, Greenwood said, and go through his suitcase as well. The FBI found just what anyone would expect in a travel bag—including the coat and gloves. There was no weapon, and no trace evidence was found on the clothing to indicate a recently fired handgun.

"Why had the duke visited Olsen?" asked Father Brown.

"He was trading gossip," Greenwood said. "He gave Olsen dossiers on three leading Members of Parliament. We found the three folders on Olsen's desk—full of scandal and dishonor. In return, Olsen gave the duke a folder on the Tsergovian royal family with a promise not to publish certain unsavory facts about them. It was a sordid business, but having made the deal, the duke then had no motive for murdering Olsen. Anyhow, as fantastic as it may sound, the true killer was hiding in a suitcase."

Father Brown sat quietly, a frown growing gradually on his wrinkled face. "I think you should leave aside the fantastic and just look at the plain facts," he said at last.

"What facts?" Greenwood asked.

"Check the duke's airplane flight—a list of passengers if there is such a thing and if it still exists. I think one of the duke's friends must have been on that plane. Identical suitcases and duplicate clothing are easily obtained. I think the two men exchanged suitcases. I think the friend continued on to the airplane's next destination with the suitcase that held the weapon and the tainted clothing.

"Your duke walked into Olsen's office," Father Brown continued, "shot the man, took the dossier on the Tsergovian royal family, and left the other dossiers with the information about our three ignoble British MPs. Then he opened his suitcase and took out a slightly smaller suitcase, the one with the breathing tubes, and one that he had persuaded a little person to recline in for a sufficient period of time. Perhaps it was one of the duke's own nephews. He positioned the rope ladder at the open window, and then he walked out the front door to hail a taxicab."

"But why bother with the three British MPs' dossiers if his intention was murder?" Greenwood said.

"Insurance," said Father Brown.

Two weeks later, Greenwood telephoned Father Brown from London. "Your surmise was entirely right," The inspector said. "The duke's head of security was on that flight and he continued on to Pittsburgh, presumably with the duke's suitcase. But tell me what led you to the truth so quickly, Father Brown?"

"I'm partial to dwarfs, being very nearly one myself," said the priest with a laugh. "And I was quite certain that the suitcase with the peepholes was nothing more than a red herring dragged across your path. Really, Inspector, you had only the duke's word that he and Olsen had come to an agreement, and

I thought it unlikely that the duke would trust a professional gossip or come to terms with him. Do you really believe he would take that risk?"

"I see now that he wouldn't," said Greenwood, "and you were also right about the insurance. The contents of those three dossiers would be made public in the event of a trial, and so we have been forbidden to prosecute the Duke of Tsergovia."

"Ah, yes," said Father Brown, "and if I may put it so, Inspector, yours was the paradox of being unable to act, not because you were ignorant, because you were the man who knew too much."

The Snow

I HAVE AN OPINION ABOUT THESE AMATEUR THEATRICALS," Sheriff Dirks said. "I say married people shouldn't be in them unless both husband and wife are in them together. Otherwise, you've got married people acting like single people, rehearsing together night after night after night. Before you know it, they're jumping into—well, Father Brown, I apologize. I wouldn't want to say something crude within the walls of a parish rectory."

"We once referred to such things," the old priest answered mildly, "as near occasions of sin."

The two men were enjoying their drinks in the parlor of the rectory. Father Brown had his cup of hot tea and the sheriff his glass of cold diet cola, beverages to which each man seemed inordinately devoted.

"The reason I'm bringing this to you, Father," Dirks continued, "is that you once told me motive is the key to every crime."

"It was hardly an original observation," said the priest. "But please continue."

"Anyway," Dirks said, "my old deputy and friend Jack Simms has been a licensed private detective since his car accident and injury." The priest nodded. "It's mostly divorce work. Snooping, really, but combined with his disability pension it's a living."

The sheriff went on to explain that Jim Fry's wife was in one of those theatricals. She was a professional dancer years ago, a ballerina. According to Dirks, Jim thought his wife might be getting too chummy with one of the actors. Jim had to go on a business trip, so he hired Jack Simms to watch her.

"Before you know it," Dirks continued, "Jack finds himself parked in front of the actor's residence at midnight. A light snow had been falling constantly ever since he got there. The snow, it turns out, is the important thing.

"It was a quiet night and Jack says he heard shouting, so he got out of his car, and he says he tried to peek through the window where there's a gap in the drapes. He says he saw the actor lying in a heap on the floor. He found a pay phone and called us, and then he waited on the front stoop until a couple of my deputies showed up. Anyway, that's his story. The deputies broke in and found the actor dead with his skull bashed in, apparently hit from behind with a brass paperweight.

"Then the deputies circled the house at a distance looking for footprints in the snow. There were none, unless you count the prints made by Jack Simms, the deputies themselves, and the cat."

"The cat?" said Father Brown.

"The cat was sitting at the back door, Father, with one set of his prints leading away from the door and another set coming back."

"Where had the cat been?" the priest asked.

"He had walked through the back yard and down the alley to the street, and then he walked back to the house."

"A busy street?"

"Well, yeah," Dirks replied impatiently.

"Why weren't the cat prints obliterated by the falling snow?" asked Father Brown.

"It wasn't so heavy of a snowstorm," said Dirks, "and the prints leading back to the house were fresh. The older prints that led away from the house were partly filled with snow, so you couldn't make out the individual toe prints, but you could see they were animal tracks and not human footprints."

The sheriff stood up and began pacing back and forth, his long legs taking him the length of the parlor in four strides. "But the point is, Father," he said, "we have a dead man, and the snow proves that only one person was at that house at that time. If June Fry had been there too, as Jack claims, then she must have flown away on a broomstick like a witch. No, Jack Simms did it. My problem is that I can't find even a hint of a motive. And, since I know your ability to puzzle these things out, Father, I was hoping you could tell me the *why* of it."

"I don't think he did it," the priest answered. "I prefer something that seems physically impossible to something as morally improbable as a deliberate murder without a motive. The lady's escape may seem impossible, but it isn't impossible in logic. She was a dancer, and dancers are athletic. Perhaps she climbed through a window and clambered up to hide herself on the roof. She might have jumped onto a tree and then leaped a great distance from the house."

"Well, Father Brown," said Dirks, returning to his chair and sitting again, "I don't buy any of that, and I seriously doubt that you do either."

"No," said Father Brown, "I don't."

"Will you tell me what you do believe?" Dirks asked.

The priest let out a long sigh. "I suppose I must," he said. "I can't have you charging poor Simms with this thing." After a long pause, he continued. "William Congreve had hold of a truth when he said 'Hell has no fury like a woman scorned'.

That is your motive, Sheriff, and it has nothing to do with snow. When someone like Mrs. Fry is overcome with fury or wrath and commits a crime of violence, usually there is remorse in the aftermath. But sometimes—"

"Sometimes?" said Dirks.

"Sometimes an act of violence is followed by a kind of hellish cunning and clarity of thought. And I dare say that does have to do with the snow." Then, seeming to change the subject, Father Brown asked, "Sheriff, can you learn what clothing this lady was wearing last evening?"

"Certainly," said Dirks.

"I assume you can somehow contrive to get possession of her coat, and I suppose that your science people can find minute particles and the like?" The sheriff nodded. "I think this will show that Mrs. Fry has been carrying that cat."

"If so, it proves nothing against her," said Dirks.

"It tells you how she left the house," Father Brown said. "She calmly and quickly took her ballet slippers from her rehearsal bag, laced them on, picked up the cat, and left the house through the back door. She walked through the snow on her toes. She was careful to take small steps, like a cat. When she reached the thoroughfare, she dropped the cat, and the cat returned home. That was the cunning and the clarity of thought I mentioned to you."

Dirks jumped to his feet. "I'll have another look at the photos of those paw prints," he said, "and then I think I am going to make an arrest."

"And I," said the priest, "am going to have a talk with Mr. Jim Fry." Then, responding to the sheriff's puzzled look, he added, "Mr. Fry once made a vow that he would love and cherish his wife for better and for worse. I want to remind him of the meaning of the word *worse*."

Kelly's Diamond Ring

KELLY SWORE HIS PALS AT THE RED LION TO SECRECY. Then he pulled a small box from his shirt pocket. It held the biggest diamond in the most expensive looking setting any of them had ever seen or had even imagined. Kelly explained his simple plan: a Saturday night date with Louise, a fancy dinner at a snooty French bistro, and then with the desserts and the brandy, well, let the trumpets sound! His extravagance surprised his pals. It contradicted Kelly's lifelong reputation as a miserly Scrooge.

"I figured if I'm going to be a good husband," Kelly said, seeing the astonishment on their faces, "I should try being a better man."

"Have the paramedics on call," Jerry said, "so they can work on Louise after her heart attack."

"Very funny," Kelly said. "Everybody's a comedian."

"Better send half of them to Louise's mother's house," said Art.

"Since you are such wise guys," Kelly said with a scowl that changed into a broad grin, "well, then, the drinks are on me."

"Now I'm gonna have the heart attack," Jerry said, clutching his chest.

"Ha, ha, ha," Kelly said.

"It's that old priest," said Art. "He's put the whammy on the poor guy."

"Very funny," said Kelly.

Kelly owned a gravel pit and managed the concern from the sprawling office he had erected near his weight station. On the afternoon of the theft, the place was warm and stuffy, as was usual for August. Kelly could have opened the window and door for a cooling cross breeze, but the dump trucks rumbling in and out of the gravel pit filled the air with dust, and Kelly suffered from allergies. He rarely opened the window. He didn't even own a doorstop.

Sam, the accountant for the enterprise, came in for a session with Kelly and the financial records.

"Hey, Boss," Sam said. "The rumor is you're getting engaged."

"People talk too damn much," Kelly said.

"It's true then?"

"Yeah," he admitted. "Here, get a load of this, Sam." Kelly took the small jewelry box out of his shirt pocket and handed it over."

Sam's eyes bulged out at the sight. "This is spectacular," he said. "Maybe you better have Doctor Crawford on hand for—"

"Everybody's a comedian," Kelly said. "Let's get to work before I decide I need a new bookkeeper. Finding a better one than you would be easy enough."

"Can't we get some fresh air in here?" Sam asked. "It's so stuffy I don't believe I can think straight." It was a frequent debate between the two and one Sam seldom won. This time he pointed out that the morning's rain shower was keeping the dust down; and, as it was Friday afternoon, truck traffic would be minimal. Kelly gave in.

"Get the window, Boss," Sam said, putting the jewelry box on Kelly's cluttered desk. "I'll get the door."

Sam propped open the door and turned back to the desk. Kelly had swiveled around in his chair and was leveling his .40-caliber Smith and Wesson at him.

"Sit down there while I close that door," Kelly said. "Hand over the ring and do it now." The small box on the desk was open. The ring was gone.

"Is this a joke?" Sam asked. "I don't have your ring."

"Have it your way," Kelly said. He reached for the phone.

◼   ◼   ◼

That evening, Sheriff Dirks was welcomed into St. Dominic's rectory by his elderly friend Father Brown, a man who had a special genius for solving the kind of puzzles that so often baffled the younger man. He was also the kind of friend who never failed to offer refreshment to his visitors.

"Thank you, that would be great," Dirks said, in response to an inquiry from Mrs. James, and then to the priest he said, "I have to find the answer fast, Father. There's a limit to how long I can hold Sam on suspicion."

"Perhaps he's not guilty," Father Brown said. "Might not the ring have been lost somewhere in that office?"

"He may not be guilty," Dirks conceded. "The first thing I told Kelly was that he had no right to point a loaded firearm at one of his employees."

"I've gotten to know Kelly quite well recently," Father Brown said. "He can be, shall we say, unpredictable."

"But here's the big problem," Dirks continued. "There's not enough time. Sam was standing there with the jewelry box, the two had a brief discussion about fresh air, and then Sam put the box down on Kelly's desk and went to the door. While he was crossing the room, Kelly looked in the box, saw the ring was gone, and reached into his drawer for his pistol. Sam opened the door, turned around, and was looking down the barrel. We're talking seconds, not minutes."

Dirks gratefully accepted the ice-cold stein of lager Mrs. James offered; then he continued his story. "I told Sam he could agree to be searched right then or he could be searched after he was booked for grand theft. He said I could search him right there on the spot. I'm not an amateur, Father Brown. He did not have the ring."

"Could he have tossed it onto a shelf? Or flung it out the door?"

"Nope," Dirks said. "We raked through the whole scene, like with a fine comb. Anyhow, Kelly told Sam to gather his belongings and never come back to the gravel pit ever again. We both watched every move as he packed some stuff in a carton. He didn't have much to take with him. Then I took him downtown."

Father Brown became silent and simply stared at the floor through his large round spectacles—a sure sign to the sheriff that the priest's brain was working in high gear, and Dirks knew better than to interrupt these reveries. Finally, Father Brown blinked his gray eyes owlishly, and said, "Sheriff, I have a mental picture of Sam closing the door with Kelly holding the gun on him. So, whether I can help you or not depends on how you answer a question. Was there a doorstop packed in the carton that Sam had taken with him?"

"Oh my good gravy," Dirks said. "I think I see where this is going. And I'm heading down to the jail."

An hour later Dirks telephoned the rectory with the news that he had found the ring among Sam's belongings. There was a small slit cut into the wedge-shaped rubber doorstop, and Sam had pushed the ring through the slit into the hollow inside.

"Sam played his boss like a piano," Dirks said. "And get this. He wasn't after the ring for its value. It was disgust and exasperation. Sam was sick of Kelly's bullying ways, and he just wanted his innings."

When Kelly learned that Sam had robbed him out of ill feeling rather than greed, he was horrified. He refused to bring charges against the man and asked him to come back to work. He apologized for his bad behavior over the years and gave Sam a long-overdue raise in pay. The rumor among Sam's friends was that Father Brown was behind this change of heart.

Whether that were true or not, the next time the sheriff spoke with Father Brown, he told the priest that he had asked Louise how she liked the kinder and more generous man Kelly had become or was trying to become.

"And what did the lady say?" Father Brown asked.

"She said, 'You bet.' She said, 'And *how!*'"

The Locked Barn

SHERIFF DIRKS WALKED WEARILY UP THE STEPS TO THE rectory front door and rang the bell. Mrs. James, the housekeeper, welcomed him warmly, and showed him into the parlor where his friend Father Brown was, as the sheriff put it, counting his beads.

To the housekeeper's question Dirks' answer was, "Oh yes, Mrs. James, I would kill for a beer." The beverage arrived just as Father Brown was crossing himself. He laid his rosary on an end table.

"Why, Sheriff," the old priest said with some concern, "you look tired, unhappy, and—if I may say so—you have discouragement written all over your face."

"I've had a tough day," Dirks replied, "and a long one, and I guess it shows."

The sheriff's day had been exasperating in more ways than he had dreamed possible. It was a sad thing that an argument had gotten out of hand, and someone, a stranger, had fatally shot a local farmer. It was frustrating to Dirks that he had been just minutes or even seconds too late to prevent the tragedy; and then he had failed to make an arrest because the killer had mysteriously slipped past the guards posted to prevent the man's escape.

Father Brown nodded in sympathy. "Earlier today," he said, "I heard about it from that part-time ambulance driver, Phil Riggs. It appears you have a double murder on your hands."

"No," Dirks said. "Not a double murder. It's a single murder and a double mystery." He then explained to Father Brown how a midmorning phone call had sent him and a deputy out to the truck farm owned and operated by Clara and Jay Means. Clara had told Dirks that her husband was in a furious argument with some man, and she was afraid they would come to blows. When Dirks arrived, he found Clara wringing her hands in front of the enormous tool barn Jay used as a combination storage facility, warehouse, and parking garage for farm equipment.

"They took their argument in there," Clara said. "The door is barred."

As the two policemen neared the barn, they heard the sounds of a noisy quarrel coming from inside the building. Two men were shouting. Then they heard the gunshot.

"Get around to the back, Sam," Dirks ordered. "Draw your weapon." Not wasting a second, Dirks started a forklift that was parked in front of the barn; at the same time, he called his headquarters to summon all available deputies to the scene. Almost before he had clicked off the small radio, he had driven one prong of the forklift into the barn door, cracking one of the boards in half. Dirks reached through with one of his long arms and dislodged the bar.

Sam's voice crackled on the radio. "The back door's barred too, Sheriff," he said.

"Stay put, Sam," Dirks ordered. He opened the barn door and saw Jay Means lying in a spreading pool of blood. The man was dead. Gun smoke hung in the gloomy air, and a pistol lay near the body. The two bare light bulbs suspended from the ceiling did not give much in the way of illumination, and so Dirks probed the interior with his flashlight. The killer was hiding somewhere inside this barn—but where? It was a big place and unbelievably cluttered.

But now it was evening, and the sheriff was beginning to relax a little and to enjoy his beer. He told Father Brown that the barn had just the two doors, front and back, and no windows. Since both doors had been barred from the inside, the killer must have been inside when Dirks broke in. There was no practical way to rig the rear door so that the bar would fall into place after someone had left by that exit. It could not be done without some sort of locking device on the inside, and there was no sign of such a thing. There were hundreds of places inside the barn where a man might hide. Dirks had ordered a systematic search, and both doors were closely watched. After almost an hour had passed in fruitless searching, Dirks sent for a pair of hounds. The hounds found nothing. Long after the medical examiner had left, and the farmer's body had been consigned to Phil Riggs' ambulance and driven to the undertaker, Dirks finally had to admit that he had been outsmarted.

At least he had a good description of the quarrelsome stranger whom Clara had seen enter the barn with her husband. The man would be found, but Dirks also had the embarrassment of two doors barred from the inside and a killer obviously trapped somewhere in the barn. Trained men had been stationed at both doors. Not so much as a field mouse had left that building, and yet no arrest had been made.

Father Brown stared at the floor for a very long moment, while Dirks scratched his head and pulled on his mustache. In truth, the priest was making up his mind whether this was the best time to let the poor man in on the truth. At length he began.

"Well, Sheriff," he said, "you may find this hard to believe, but I know how your man got out of that barn."

"You know?" Dirks said, shaking his head. "How could you? You weren't even there."

"That is true enough," said Father Brown, "but you have always told me I am a good listener. I find it easy to listen, because people have such interesting things to say. I told you a moment ago that I had a chat with Phil Riggs earlier today, and he told me about driving the ambulance out to that barn to fetch the body this afternoon. He said that your Deputy, Gene, had the front door closely guarded."

"So, Phil and Gene know how the guy got out?"

"Not exactly," Father Brown said. "You assume they have the same facts you do, Sheriff, but you didn't explain things to Phil. You just told him what to do. All he knows is what he saw, and he knows nothing about what you saw. Phil Riggs had no idea there was any mystery in the business. He wasn't talking about an impossible escape or the fugitive who got away. He just talked about a double killing. It was a natural assumption, I guess, since he had wheeled two corpses out of the barn on his gurney."

"I already told you there weren't two corpses, Father," Dirks said with exasperation.

"I know," said Father Brown. "One of those corpses was not a corpse. Oh my goodness, Sheriff! I'll ask Mrs. James to bring you a towel. Will you be all right? It is certainly not like you to spill your beer."

The Photograph

SHERIFF DIRKS KNEW HE HAD MISSED SOMETHING. He knew this with a powerful feeling of certitude. Yet he had not the slightest inkling of what it was he had missed. His wife Marie had suggested he pay another visit to Father Brown. "He'll give your mind a jolt," she said.

"I'll do just that," said Dirks, "but I hope nobody in the department ever finds out I'm completely dependent on a Catholic priest for expert criminological advice."

Sheriff Dirks had always enjoyed the slow pace of the small community he served. Lately, however, the county seemed to be getting more than its share of sensational crimes—the kind that make splashy newspaper headlines.

When a vacationing state senator named Hack was stabbed to death in a local hotel, the pace picked up considerably. The senator had been single, or rather divorced; he was staying alone in the hotel because, as his staff told the police, he needed a break from the hectic legislative pace. The problem was that no one could be found who had seen or heard anything suspicious.

All elected officials get death threats from time to time, and the FBI was tracing that sort of lead; by a stroke of unbelievably good luck, a key bit of evidence turned up a week after the murder. It was provided by a tourist whose own room had been near Senator Hack's room.

The tourist was a shutterbug who had snapshots of practically everyone he had met on his vacation and nearly everything he had seen. His room was identical to the one rented by Hack, but identical in reverse, for the furnishings along the north wall in one room were duplicated along the south wall in the other. The two balconies faced one another across a small atrium, and so the tourist had taken some pictures of the senator's room, thinking it would show a likeness of his own room from a different perspective. One of these shots had shown the divan in Hack's room; something looked suspicious in the large mirror that in these layouts is always to be found above the divan. The FBI's photographic enhancements showed a man who wore a patch over his left eye. He was wielding a knife in his right hand.

Because the image was seen in a mirror, of course the knife wielder was actually left handed, and the patch would have covered his right eye. Witnesses remembered seeing a dark-haired man with a black eye-patch in the hotel lobby, and Dirks was confident that with this new description the killer would be found, especially with the resources and help of the feds. That had been three months ago; after every plausible lead had been chased down, there was no suspect in view.

As Dirks stepped into the parlor of St. Dominic's rectory, Father Brown, being quite short in stature, had to crane his neck to look the sheriff in the face. He offered the taller man a glass of claret.

"I'm not sure," Dirks said, as he collapsed into a chair and pulled at his gray mustache. "I don't know if I'm on duty or not. You see, I've come to get your opinion on another murder case I can't seem to figure out."

"The murder of that senator?"

"Well, of course, you've seen the newspapers," Dirks said. "And, yes, Father Brown, I think I could do with a small glass of wine."

After Mrs. James had served them both a generous glass of Bordeaux, which Father Brown insisted on calling "claret," Dirks described his problem without further interruption.

Father Brown said nothing at first but fixed the sheriff with his gaze, thought for a moment, and then asked, "Do you know the exact location of the camera when that photo was taken?"

"Sure," Dirks said, "in a general way. It's pretty obvious."

"But I mean the exact location and position of that camera," said Father Brown. "I think an expert could help you by studying the lines of perspective, but I'm not really up-to-date on such things. If you learn anything from the experiment, come back here and we'll talk about it." With that the priest excused himself, declaring that he had promised to work on something for the pastor and he had better see to it without further procrastination. Leaning on his knobby cane, he escorted Dirks to the door with a cheerful, "Good evening, Sheriff, and my best regards to Mrs. Dirks."

For once, the sheriff had not been impressed with the old priest's suggestion, but having no better ideas, he did as he had been asked.

It was a month before he again found himself in the parlor room of St. Dominic's rectory. "You *are* a wizard, Father Brown," he said. "Don't try to deny it. The man who stabbed Senator Hack has been identified, located, arrested, indicted, and is awaiting trial. The guy wasn't interested in politics. He was a jealous husband."

Father Brown did not seem surprised by this information. "My advice helped you then?" he asked.

"Oh, yes," Dicks said, "after I took a couple of wrong turns. The FBI photo experts told us the picture had been taken through a zoom lens that was just a bit too far away from the senator's room to have been snapped from inside the tourist's room. So I thought maybe we had a picture of an unrelated knifing incident somewhere else in the hotel. We soon saw that idea wouldn't fly. Then we decided the snapshot was part of a misdirection ploy, and that maybe this tourist with the camera was an accomplice. But we got it right, finally."

"Congratulations."

"How did you *know*, Father?" Dirks asked.

"I believe it was a simple matter of logic," said the priest. "I had to assume that your description of the killer was inaccurate or else you would have found him. I saw only one way in which that could be true. It was not a watertight deduction, but it is the best I could do with the facts you gave me. I had to reason from the premise that the fugitive was not wearing a patch over his right eye."

"It's obvious in hindsight," Dirks said. "Of course, that stupid tourist guy admits that he forgot but—oh, yes—now he remembers framing the picture in his mirror, so that the image would be reversed and the layout would match his own room. That's why the room seemed just that much farther away, and of course the image of the killer was reversed twice—once in our tourist's mirror and again in Senator Hack's mirror. We went back to a suspect we had previously questioned, a man with an eye patch. We had cleared him because we thought his patch covered the wrong eye. But, listen, Father Brown, how can I ever thank you?"

The priest smiled benignly. "Thank me by promising to come back here at the end of your day so that we can properly toast your success with a bit of Father Bell's excellent claret."

With the exception of "till death do us part," it was the sincerest and happiest promise Dirks had ever made.

Teamwork

SHERIFF DIRKS FELL INTO THE CHAIR AND TRIED TO RUB the fatigue out of his eyes. He looked at his elderly friend and murmured, "Well, I've done it again. There's been another impossible escape on my watch."

The friend, Father Brown, was always ready to help Dirks with his puzzles. Although the priest was in his nineties, he was in good health and had lost none of his ability to explain confusing facts in new and unexpected ways.

"Would you like a cup of coffee?" the older man asked. "I'm going to have a cup of tea." They were seated at a small table in the kitchen of St. Dominic's rectory, which seemed especially cheery this morning with the sun streaming in through the windows over the sink.

"No coffee, thanks," said Dirks. "I just want to tell you about this crazy situation south of town."

"I'd like to hear about it, of course."

"It's Zeke Freeman," Dirks began, "a young construction worker with a reputation for a hot temper. He's been conducting a stormy romance with Dora Cole, a divorcée who lives on the edge of town out by the canal. We had a 9-1-1 phone call from Dora this afternoon. She said Zeke was in a rage and trying to break into her house." Dirks went on to describe how he had rushed to the scene with three deputies. By the time they arrived, Zeke was standing at the front door with Doris in front of him. He was holding a handgun up against her head.

"Dora's house is a small one-story, two-bedroom ranch at the end of a street," Dirks explained. "There's no basement, and the layout is basically a simple square. As far as anything nearby, there's a neighbor on one side, the canal is on the other side, and a field of brush lies behind. I sent Sam to watch on the neighbor's side, Gene to guard the canal, and John to keep an eye on the rear."

"Did you keep this Zeke fellow in sight while they took up their positions?" Father Brown asked.

"Of course, I did, Father," Dirks said. "Otherwise you'd say Zeke beat it out through the back door before we got set, but then there wouldn't be any mystery in the business at all." Father Brown nodded. "Anyhow," said Dirks, "what happened next was this. Zeke shut the door, and I waited a minute or two, and then I took a look through the front window. I saw Dora lying on the floor.

"About this time another squad pulled up, so I made sure the house was extra well surrounded before two of us popped in through the front door. Dora was alive but knocked silly. It turns out Zeke had banged her on the back of her head with the butt end of his pistol.

"But here's the point of the story. The long and short of it is that Zeke just plain vanished. He was not hiding in the house, and my guys all swear he didn't get past them. I haven't a clue as to how he disappeared, and so I'm left with egg all over my face. It seems to me that for a sheriff in a sleepy small town, I've been getting more than my share of egg lately."

"And that is the whole story?" Father Brown asked. "There's nothing more?"

"That's it, except that the Indiana state police picked Zeke up an hour ago near Lafayette."

"I'm sorry, Sheriff," Father Brown said, "but the only possible answer is that one of your men allowed Zeke to escape."

"I can't accept that, Father," Dirks said. "None of my guys is a friend of Zeke's, and they don't hang out with him. Zeke's friends are in the building trades, and he runs with the hard-drinking crew."

"I see your point," Father Brown conceded. "Your men would have no motive for helping Zeke."

"It's more than that," Dirks said. "It's the idea of loyalty. My young deputies have it. You can tell. You work with them, and you weed out the ones who don't naturally accept loyalty as a code to live by." Seeing the priest's doubtful expression, Dirks decided to explain the point further.

"When I took over from Sheriff Morley," he said, "the department was undermanned, and I had to build it back up. I took on local boys, mostly. They know the community. I was a basketball player when I was a kid, and I looked for guys who played sports in high school. I especially like boys who played contact sports like football and wrestling. They know about discipline, and they have a natural toughness about them. They've learned teamwork and the idea of being loyal to the team. A police force is a kind of team, you know, and so teamwork and loyalty are things I insist on."

It seemed there was nothing more to be said, but as usual, Father Brown had a totally unexpected approach for Dirks. The sheriff accepted the strange assignment simply because he had no other leads to follow.

The next evening Dirks paid another call on Father Brown, this time accepting the cup of coffee Mrs. James offered. "You *are* a wizard," Dirks said. "You are simply a magician."

Father Brown laughed and shook his head. "I hope it's more a matter of reasoning," he said, "than magic or wizardry."

"I went to the high school, just as you suggested," Dirks said, "and I looked at the yearbook for the year when Zeke was a senior. Not only were Zeke and my man John in the same graduating class, but they were co-captains of the football team." Father Brown merely nodded at these revelations.

"I confronted John with this," Dirks said. "I told him I wasn't going to charge him with aiding and abetting, just as long as he agreed to a fast career change. He handed me his badge." The sheriff sat for a while just shaking his head. "How did you know?" he asked.

"You told me that your deputies are loyal men," said Father Brown, "but your story about Zeke's escape showed that one of them was disloyal. The only way to reconcile these facts is to conclude that you had a deputy who was loyal to something other than your police force. I thought it might be a school connection, even though all that should have ended with their commencement years ago. I suppose that in John's eyes, his school football comrades will always be his team."

Dirks started to reply, but he stopped with his mouth half open, the light of a new understanding dawning in his eyes. "The team," he said slowly. "I guess it's not so much being loyal as what you're loyal to."

Father Brown's reply was as sincere as it was simple.

"Amen," he said.

The News

S HERIFF DIRKS HAD FALLEN INTO THE HABIT OF CALLING on Father Brown to discuss his dilemmas. The priest was more than a good listener and sounding board, for—despite advancing old age—he could be depended upon to suggest a new direction when the investigation seemed to have reached a dead end.

That is why Father Brown thought Dirks would return his phone call, even though the sheriff was up to his neck in a murder case that had interrupted what had been shaping up as a quiet and even sleepy kind of summer. Father Brown would not have put it this way, but in truth he was too valuable a resource for the sheriff to ignore.

The priest returned to the front page of the local Sunday newspaper he had spread out on the table before him. He studied the lurid headline: "Professor Shot to Death in Apartment Elevator." Then he reread the first paragraph:

The lifeless body of journalism professor Max Loren was discovered by two security guards in the Wilson Arms apartment building Saturday morning at 5:00 AM. The police, who were on the scene almost immediately, said the victim had been shot in the head mere seconds before the elevator in which he had been descending opened at the lobby floor.

Father Brown smiled at the way the reporter had crammed so much information into his lead sentences. Yet he was saddened by Loren's death and not least because he had been a regular reader of the professor's weekly column. It was devoted to exposing the hidden political biases in news reporting, and this made Loren the kind of crusading reformer that the priest had always admired.

Father Brown wanted to ask Sheriff Dirks if the reporter who had written the news story about this sensational murder had gotten his facts right, and he reread the story as he waited for Dirks' call. In the lobby, the guards had heard something that sounded like a muffled gunshot coming from just above the bank of elevator doors. Almost immediately, an elevator car arrived at ground floor level, the door opened, and they saw the professor's body dressed in a jogging suit and lying sprawled on the floor. There was what looked like a bullet hole in the man's left temple, and a smell of gunpowder lingered in the air. The guards told the reporter that the professor always went out for a jog at five on Saturday mornings.

The Wilson Arms was a small apartment building, and it was unusual in that there were so few exits. The garage for its residents was in a separate building across the street, and except for the emergency fire doors, the only way in or out was through the lobby. It was a spacious lobby with a glass front and five doors that opened onto the sidewalk and the street.

In less than a minute after the discovery of the body, one of the security guards had flagged down a passing squad car; in five minutes more, the building was under the control of sheriff's deputies. The security guards swore that after the gunshot and before the police arrived no one had entered or left the building through the lobby doors.

The deputies immediately cordoned off the place and allowed no one to enter. Those leaving had to show their identification and, as you would expect at that early hour, they were all residents of the building. The police also searched every possible hiding place, canvassed the apartments, and checked the stairwells. It was evident that the alarms on the fire doors were in working order and that none of those doors had been opened at any time in the recent past. Sheriff Dirks was quoted as saying the killer had to be a resident of the building and, although gathering depositions would be a time-consuming process, in the end the guilty party would be identified.

The rectory phone rang, and sure enough, it was the sheriff. "Can you make it quick, Father?"

"I think so, Sheriff. I've just one question and then one request."

"Shoot," Dirks said.

"I've been reading about the murder in the Sunday *Sentinel*. Tell me, is this reporter, Joe Gains, reliable?"

"Yeah, I read it," Dirks answered. "Joe's got his facts right. He's the main city hall man, and maybe he's too tight with the mayor to be unbiased in his political reporting, but he's always been reliable on police news. That's why I didn't toss him out when I found him interviewing everybody in that lobby."

"If Joe Gains has the facts right," Father Brown said, "then I believe I have the facts right, too."

"So, have you cracked the case?" Dirks said, thinking this was a little joke.

"Yes," Father Brown said. "I have." There was silence at Dirks' end of the line. "Here's what you I want you to do, Sheriff. Check every resident of the Wilson Arms who gave a party or entertained guests Friday night."

"You think a guest waited all night for Loren to go jogging? Then how'd he get out of the building?" But Father Brown, believing he had done his duty in justice to the memory of Professor Loren, had already rung off.

Dirks called Father Brown back at ten that evening. "You are truly a wonder," he said, "but now that I know who he is, tell me how I'm going to convict the guy."

"I can guess at the motive," Father Brown replied. "If you get into the professor's files, I think you will find he was going to expose some illegal goings on in our municipal government. I imagine the professor's killer was in that business 'up to his neck', if I may be permitted an Americanism. But anyway, when you decided to let Joe Gains stay in that lobby to get his newspaper story, it might have been well for you to have asked your men which one of them let him in."

"I see that now," Dirks said. "The dinner party broke up at about midnight. Joe probably spent the night in the stairwell. He was waiting for the professor when he went out for his jog. It looks like he shot him and hopped off the elevator at the second floor. When the place filled up with deputies, I guess he just popped out into the lobby from the entrance to the stairwell and started interviewing them. He must have had the murder weapon right there in one of his pockets. And it's ironic, Father, that except for you, he'd have gotten away with it."

"The irony is this," replied Father Brown. "Except for his superior reporting abilities, I would never have learned the facts that pointed right at him."

The Meaning of "Omit"

S HERIFF DIRKS ENJOYED SERVING AS CHIEF LAW OFFICER in the small town and surrounding rural countryside that were Bardo County. Most of his work was routine, of course, but for reasons he could not fathom, he seemed to have more than his share of the sort of sensational crimes that make headlines. Luckily for the sheriff, he could always take his most perplexing problems to his wise friend, Father Brown.

One of his most bewildering cases had come to light when the nurse who visited Perry Melrose every afternoon found the old gentleman dead in his kitchen. She had grown very fond of Mr. Melrose. Although he was gradually losing his battle with diabetes, she found him unfailingly cheerful and kind. He insisted on paying her twice the going rate for visiting nurses. In truth, he was a lonely man, and he was eager for her company.

On her final visit to his townhouse, Nurse Smith was much more than saddened to find him dead—she was shocked and appalled. Melrose was lying on the floor by the glass door that leads from the kitchen to the patio, his throat gruesomely slashed, and his old-fashioned straight razor lying near him on the floor. The nurse assumed he had taken his own life in this grisly way, and it was obvious to her that he had been dead for several hours. Perhaps it had been as long ago as the night before.

What she saw next added greatly to her distress. Melrose had reached up with his last strength to write something on the door, smearing a word there in block letters with his own blood. The word was "omit." He must have been in great pain when he did this, and the very meaninglessness of the word horrified Nurse Smith. Despite her experience with physical trauma, the scene made her feel nauseous.

As soon as she had composed herself, she called the sheriff's department. Sheriff Dirks was not long in arriving at the townhouse, and he quickly dismissed the idea of suicide. His deputy had found the man's wallet on the kitchen floor with the folding money gone. Furthermore, someone had rifled Melrose's desk; if there had been anything of value there, which was likely, it had been carried off. In the bedroom, the dresser and closet had the appearance of having been searched by someone in a hurry.

Nurse Smith had nothing very helpful to contribute. She told Dirks she came daily to measure Melrose's vital signs, to test his blood sugar, and to administer an insulin shot if that were indicated. Recently he had made the decision, after conferring with his doctor, to give up the townhouse and move into a nursing home.

The nurse had no inkling as to who might have so brutally murdered her patient. When he talked about his friends, she said, it was always, sadly enough, in the past tense. He had no relatives, at least not here. He had a son in Phoenix whom, she thought, sometimes had telephoned; but he visited rarely, if ever.

"Which nursing home, Sheriff?"

Dirks was discussing the case with the priest whose powers of deduction and knowledge of the human heart had helped him on so many occasions in the past. He thought a solution to the present case would be out of the reach of even Father Brown's genius, however. The visit would be a pleasant one, regardless of the practical result, for the rectory boasted an endless supply of very fine Bordeaux.

"Shady Manor Senior Care Center," Dirks answered. "Why?"

"I know the four homes near here," the priest answered. "Father Bell and I have friends to visit in them and priestly duties to perform. I know it can cost a fortune to stay at Shady Manor. This Melrose must have been a wealthy man."

"He had the big bucks, for sure," Dirks said; "and his son is his only heir, so he stands to inherit the whole of it. He hasn't been informed yet."

"Oh?"

"Yeah, he's traveling on vacation in the Far East," Dirks said. "We've tried to get word to him through the State Department, but we don't know exactly where he is."

"Well, it was Saint Augustine," Father Brown replied, "who said God judges it better to bring good out of evil than to prevent evil from existing. The son would not have inherited much of anything if his father had lived to spend his last years at Shady Rest. The residents there end up assigning all their savings to the institution, which then promises to take care of their every earthly need until death. I hope the son uses his new wealth wisely. But do you really have no suspects, no leads?"

"We have zip, zero, and zilch," Dirks said, "except for the word he wrote on the door, and I haven't a clue as to what that means. It isn't an acronym like OPEC. I've been to the dictionaries and the phrase books to see if 'omit' is the beginning of a longer word or phrase. But that was a dead end."

"Literally a dead end," Father Brown said. "It was his dying act. Whatever it means, it must have been of deep importance." The old priest sat silently for a few moments lost in his thoughts. Then, as if something had jolted him out of his reverie, he suddenly looked up and asked, "By the way, Sheriff, how old is Tim Melrose?"

"In his fifties," Dirks answered. Then an odd look came over his face. "Hey, what's going on, Father Brown? I never told you the son's name! How on earth did you know it was 'Tim'?"

The old priest shook his head in sadness tinged with anger. Finally, he said, "Just think of it! Tim murdered his own father to get his money! He could not abide the thought of the nursing home taking what he supposed was rightfully his. You'll be able to prove he was here at the crucial time, I suppose?"

"Airline and rental car records might tell that tale," Dirks said.

"Yes, and eventually he'll come back to claim his inheritance. Then, I imagine you'll arrest him."

"But how on earth do you know it was him?" Dirks asked.

Father Brown replied with a question of his own. "What goes on in a person's mind as he slides into eternity? In this case, Perry Melrose had something to say, and as his rapidly dimming eyes focused on that door, he reached out and wrote his message on the glass. He died before he was quite finished; and for some reason—a reason we will never discover—he wrote it to be read from the other side of the glass, from the outside, from the patio. I mean he wrote his message backwards, from right to left. From the kitchen side he seems to have written o-m-i-t, but from the patio it would read, T-I-M-O."

"—T-H-Y," Dirks finished. "Timothy."

The Pawn

IT SEEMED TO SHERIFF DIRKS THAT ALL THE EVIDENCE
pointed to Eddy O'Shea. Yet he made the arrest with great
reluctance. The sheriff's facts did not mesh with his feel-
ings, and so he decided to lay the case out for Father Brown, St.
Dominic's very old but very wise assistant pastor.

Dirks quickly reviewed the facts for his friend. Although the
ticket office closes at seven, the train depot of the small town is
kept open until midnight for the convenience of travelers. Of
course, the building is usually deserted between trains, and so
Sally Freund was surprised and horrified to find herself sharing
the waiting room with a lifeless corpse. She discovered the man
lying face down in a pool of blood, the handle of a common
kitchen knife jutting out from between his shoulder blades.
The victim was quickly identified as a local lawyer named Carl
Grimm.

The grieving Mrs. Grimm told the sheriff she had last seen
her husband no more than an hour earlier. Eddy O'Shea had
phoned, she said, and had asked, rather urgently, for Grimm
to meet him at nine that evening. He suggested the train depot
for both convenience and privacy.

For his part, O'Shea admitted going to the depot at nine, but he denied the meeting had been his idea. He claimed that Grimm, or someone pretending to be Grimm, had phoned him and insisted that they have a private talk. He said that they had indeed met at the depot; but after a minute's confusion, they had agreed that some unknown third party had played a malicious joke on them. O'Shea said that he had gone straight home then and had not harmed Grimm in any way.

"If you believe Eddy," Father Brown asked, "what compelled you to arrest him?"

"For one thing," Dirks said, "the timeline is against him. Based on what Mrs. Grimm told us, her husband would have arrived at the depot at almost exactly nine o'clock. O'Shea says he entered by the back door at nine, and immediately spotted Grimm, who seemed to have just entered through the front door. They talked for no more than two minutes, and O'Shea says he then left the building and assumed that Grimm had done the same. Sally Freund says she found the body at nine-ten. She is sure of the time, because she was very early for the 9:55 train and was expecting a long, boring wait in the station."

Dirks paused for a sip from the can of diet cola Mrs. James had found for him and then continued. "The weapon was a common kitchen knife," he said, "one with a long, thin blade. It is sold by the thousands and is impossible to trace, but Jim at Diamond's Hardware says he sold such a knife to O'Shea just last week. Now O'Shea was able to show us an identical knife in one of his kitchen drawers, but he could have bought a second knife, and that would show cunning. 'Malice aforethought' we call it."

Father Brown nodded with interest but said nothing.

"Now as to motive," Dirks said, "well, I have a sordid tale to tell. Five years ago, Eddy was having a secret love affair with Doc Case's wife—Terri, her name was. Carl Grimm found out about it, and he spilled the beans to Eddy's wife. It darned near caused the O'Shea's marriage to break up, but Eddy begged for a second chance and vowed he'd never stray again. I think he meant it, and I think they've put the pieces back together. But Eddy had every reason to hate Carl Grimm. In his mind, he might have thought he had an old score to settle."

"So Eddy O'Shea had, as you policemen say," Father Brown murmured, "opportunity, means, and motive. And no one else had them?"

"Sally Freund was there at the scene," the sheriff said, "but so far as I can find out, she didn't even know Carl Grimm."

"Well," said Father Brown, "I don't think your friend Eddie O'Shea did it."

"Really?" said Dirks. "Why?"

"His plan, if it was his plan, would put the suspicion quickly and squarely on himself. Would he do that? To make me believe O'Shea is your killer, I would have to believe that after five peaceable years, he suddenly decided to take his revenge because he saw a knife in a hardware store. I can't—oh, my."

"What is the matter, Father Brown?" Dirks asked.

"Oh, my," repeated Father Brown. "Sheriff, do you remember the last time you bought something at that hardware store? Could you say who was waiting in line at the payment counter with you?"

"Of course," Dirks said. "This is a small town and people are friendly. I could probably tell you everyone who was in the store at the time."

"Then ask that Jim fellow at the store if he can remember who was standing there when Eddy bought that knife. Ask Eddy as well. See if you can get a complete list of those who might have seen what Eddy was buying."

"Do you have anybody in mind?" asked Dirks. But the priest did not answer.

■   ■   ■

After seeing his last patient of the day, Doctor Case found Father Brown sitting in his waiting room and holding his knobby cane between his knees. "Have you an appointment?" the doctor asked.

"You saw Eddy O'Shea buy a kitchen knife," the priest said without prelude. "It gave you an idea. You bought the same knife for yourself, though surely not in that store or even in this town. You made phone calls summoning those two men to the depot, and then you hid in the shadows. When Eddy left, you used your surgeon's skill with that knife."

"And you are a senile and irresponsible old imbecile," said Case. "I have never had any quarrel with Carl Grimm. Eddy O'Shea is the one who hated him."

"Carl Grimm was just a pawn in the game you were playing, Doctor Case—a minor piece to be sacrificed. Eddy O'Shea was to be your victim, the man who had ruined your marriage. If you had simply killed Eddie, the police would have suspected you immediately. It was devilishly clever of you to plan this crime so that suspicion would fall on Eddy and that he would be convicted of a murder he did not commit."

"If there were any truth in this nonsense," the doctor answered, "I could easily arrange for you to have a heart attack right here and now."

"Such a thing would not save you, Doctor Case. The police are questioning people at the hardware store. Next they'll be asking you where you were when Grimm was stabbed."

"Then why did you come here?"

"I have come," said Father Brown, "to ask you to return to the Church and her sacraments," and he watched as the man collapsed into a chair with his face buried in his hands. Although the priest said nothing aloud, his lips never stopped moving until long after the police had taken Doctor Case away.

Ned Wilson's Palace

SHERIFF DIRKS MADE HIMSELF COMFORTABLE, AND ACcepted the glass of excellent Bordeaux, which Father Brown, in the fashion of the British, insisted on calling "claret." The sheriff was in the middle of a criminal case, and he was in over his head, but he showed good sense, as he so often did, in bringing his problem to Father Brown.

"Sheriff," said the priest, "I have lived here for several years now, and yet I have never heard of this illustrious Wilson family."

"They've always been very aloof," said Dirks. "The story is this. Nobody today remembers exactly how Great Grandfather Wilson got rich, but there is this rumor that it was something illegal. During the panic of 1908, he bought up great chunks of real estate from bankruptcies, and built a huge fortune. His heir, now referred to as Grandfather Wilson, had a big success in playing the stock market. He was one of the clever or lucky few who sold his holdings just before the market collapsed in 1929.

"That brings us to Ned Wilson III," Dirks continued, "the grandfather's only child. He went to the university in the fifties, and was shocked to find himself a social outcast. Although his family had ten times more money than any of the others, Ned was not polished. He had never learned to rumba. He did not know how to play contract bridge. He ate his peas with a knife."

"Well, I never learned the rumba," said Father Brown, laughing, "or to play bridge for that matter. I do think I mind my peas in the proper manner. And my Qs."

"After Ned graduated from law school," the sheriff continued, ignoring the pun, "his father's wealth landed him a partnership in a big law firm. Ned was a good enough attorney, but he never was able to shake off his shame over the way his peers had treated him at college. That's why he made it his life's ambition to climb to the top of the social register. His future inheritance enabled him to marry the daughter of an important family, and he saw that their two children learned the social niceties. When Grandfather Wilson died and left him the family fortune, Ned quit the practice of law to devote himself to a pet project."

The sheriff rose from his chair and continued his narrative as he paced back and forth on the carpet. "He bought a large parcel of land in the northeast corner of the county," Dirks said. "He went all out with a huge mansion, stables, ornate gardens—the works. He hired the most highly regarded butler he could find in England to serve him as a kind of head steward. The man oversaw everything from design and construction of the buildings to the hiring and training of staff. Now that I've been there, I can say the atmosphere seems very British. The butler—his name is Graves—is so British that when you lay eyes on him and hear him speak, you want stand up and sing 'God Save the Queen!' Graves must have been pained when Wilson insisted on naming his estate 'the Palace.'"

"Are you joking?" Father Brown asked. "Good heavens!"

"It was Graves who discovered the body in the library," Dirks continued. "Wilson's skull had been bashed in from behind with a fireplace poker. When we were called to come out to investigate, it was the first time I had ever seen the estate.

Wilson had his own private security staff, and he never bothered the county except for a couple of times when there was an accident and they called for the rescue squad. Wilson was sixty-eight years old and a widower."

"Why would anyone want him dead?" Father Brown asked.

"Maybe it's this," Dirks said, sitting down again. "About six months ago, Wilson settled generous annuities on his two children. Then he placed the remainder of his fortune, and it was huge, into a trust. During his lifetime, this trust was dedicated to operating his estate—insurance, taxes, upkeep, salaries, and everything. Upon his death, the trusteeship passes to the university—his alma mater. Of course, the package included ownership of the Palace. Wilson's two children aren't happy about losing their home and all the luxury that went with it."

"Do you think one of them swung that poker?" the priest asked.

"Not really, Father Brown," Dirks said. "They're too laid back. They'll regret not having cocktails by the big pool in the summer and cocktails by the big fireplace in the winter, but they just don't get all that excited about anything. Wilson's son laughs and says he wishes he had killed the old man before he gave the family fortune away, but he wouldn't bother doing it after the fact. The daughter is just kind of passively angry, if there is such a thing."

"What about the household staff?" Father Brown asked.

"They didn't know about the bequest," Dirks answered. "They hadn't been told."

"Do you know why Wilson willed his fortune to the university?" Father Brown asked.

"Yes, I do," said Dirks. "He traded it for a standing invitation to every university sponsored social event for the rest of his life. He could sit in the President's skybox at football games, he was invited to every faculty tea, and he was welcome to sit at the speaker's table at all university-sponsored dinners. Of course, he didn't attend all of these events or even most of them. He could pick and choose among them, but he was invited to everything. The university assigned a secretary to the Wilson schedule and correspondence. Given the amount of money involved, they considered it a bargain or maybe even a steal."

"Wilson was climbing his precious social ladder to the very end," said Father Brown, shaking his head in either disapproval or wonder. "One might almost excuse Graves for the fit of fury that drove him to pick up that poker."

"You mean the butler did it?" said Dirks with a laugh.

But Father Brown did not laugh. "His life's work," he said "was creating a replica of Britannia in the colonial countryside. From what you say, he did a masterful job. Then one day, Wilson casually mentioned that at his death the Palace would be turned into a common meeting center or office building. Wilson turned his back on his butler, planning simply to walk away from him. I imagine Graves saw red, as American novelists like to say. He will confess, I suspect, if you put the accusation to him strongly."

"So, you know how Graves must have felt," said Dirks, "because you and he are fellow Englishmen?"

"I knew how Graves must have felt," said Father Brown solemnly, "because he and I are fellow human beings."

The Apocrypha

T HE DEWAR MURDER IS ALL WRAPPED UP," SHERIFF
Dirks said, "but I'll be happy to give you the details, if
you're interested." Dirks was discussing one of his cases
with the elderly Catholic priest who enjoyed hearing about the
sheriff's work and who sometimes helped him think through
problems. The two were relaxing in the rectory of St. Dominic's
where, Dirks could testify, hospitality was never wanting.

"Well, the newspaper account seemed a bit garbled," said
Father Brown.

"The story isn't complicated," said Dirks. "Dewar's sister
showed up at his apartment Sunday morning expecting that
they would attend church together. When he wouldn't answer
the bell, she called the superintendent, and they found the
brother lying dead on his living room floor. His wallet was on
the floor beside his body, emptied of cash. It turns out somebody had smacked him on the side of the head with a big heavy
ashtray. But there were no prints on the ashtray or the wallet.
Both wiped clean.

"The sister said Dewar carried large amounts of cash at all
times. He was one of those guys," the sheriff continued, "who
feel naked without at least a thousand at the ready. The medical

examiner said Dewar had so much alcohol in his blood, he was drunk enough to be close to passing out without any help from ashtrays. He put the time of death at somewhere around midnight the night before.

"Now, Father Brown, I enjoy a glass of wine now and again, as you know. But mine is a minor vice. At least I don't get blitzed on Saturday night in preparation for worshiping God on Sunday morning."

Father Brown considered this. "Your glass of wine is a small evil that God might excuse," he replied. "Ours is a sacrament for which God must be praised."

"Have it your way, Father, but Doc says Dewar had enough alcohol in his blood to be way more than just legally drunk. Still, as I said before, it was the blow to the head that killed him, not the booze.

"We questioned the night doorman, and he said Dewar had come home by cab at midnight with a companion. One peculiar thing, the doorman says; Dewar might have been a touch on the tipsy side, but he was by no means staggering drunk. This tells me that they must have kept on drinking after they arrived in Dewar's apartment.

"Anyhow, the doorman was able to give us a good description because the man's appearance is so unusual. He is at least six-five in height and he has a head of flaming red hair. Only one man in the county fits that description, and that's Red Roberts."

"I don't know him," Father Brown said.

"Well, he's a Baptist," Dirks replied, by way of explanation. "Anyhow, the doorman says Red left the building just after midnight—at about twelve-twenty—and that Dewar's apartment had no other visitors before his shift was over at six. We found the cabbie who dropped Dewar off at the apartment building, and he corroborates the doorman's story. For one thing, his description of Dewar's companion fits Red Roberts to a tee.

And for another thing, the cabbie also says both men were a bit unsteady, but not totally plastered.

"Anyhow, the cabbie was waiting at the curb checking his money and his log and thinking about calling it a night when Roberts came back out of the apartment building. The cab's log puts that at twelve twenty-five in the morning, so that matches what the doorman said, and the address where the guy asked to be taken is Robert's home. Game, set, and match. We were there waiting for him when he got back from Sunday morning services."

"Did he confess to the crime?" asked Father Brown.

"No," Dirks said. "He is going to depend on his reputation as a deeply religious man of strong moral character. But, Father Brown, even a pillar of the church gets reckless when he's under the influence of alcohol."

"Did it strike you," Father Brown asked, "that whatever happened in that apartment took precious little time?" Before the sheriff could reply, Father Brown abruptly asked a new question: "Do you have a Bible at home that includes the *Apocrypha*?"

"Sure," Dirks said. "Why?"

"Have you ever read the story of Daniel and Susanna? It's the world's first detective story. It tells of two witnesses who accused a woman of a capital crime. An energetic young man named Daniel surprised everyone by treating the witnesses as suspects. He separated the two and exposed them as liars when they contradicted one another on the minor or trivial facts in the background of their story."

Sheriff Dirks sat for some moments, staring at his shoes. At length he bid his friend his heartfelt thanks and goodnight.

The sheriff returned to the rectory the following evening in a happy mood, and Mrs. James was not slow in offering him refreshment.

"Thank you," he replied. "I'll have a little of that wine Father Brown calls a sacrament."

"He calls it claret," the housekeeper said, "but it's really Bordeaux."

"A rose by any other name," said Father Brown, quoting his favorite poet.

"I got the doorman alone," Dirks said. "I asked him if, when Red Roberts came back out of the building, he had helped him find a cab. He said of course he did, because that's his job. But when I questioned the cabbie, he said the doorman had stayed put in the lobby. Then I asked both of them separately for more details about Red Roberts' appearance—what he was wearing and so on. There was nothing short of a flood of contradictions on these kinds of minor matters of detail.

"The truth is, as they finally admitted, Roberts was never at the scene. They had to assist the besotted Dewar up to his apartment—a fact they covered up by telling us he wasn't all that drunk—and then, when Dewar promptly passed out, they decided to help themselves to the cash in his wallet. When their victim came round and drunkenly confronted them, the doorman panicked and let him have it with the ashtray.

"The cabbie remembered his previous fare, an easily identifiable character he thought they could pin their crime on. So they concocted this yarn of theirs, and the cabbie changed his taxi log to fit it. As far as I'm concerned, the moral of the story is that nothing good comes of intemperance."

The priest shook his head. "Greed," he said, his eyes twinkling. "Sheriff, if you'll be so intemperate as to accept a second glass of claret, I'd like to tell you about that collection of writings you call the *Apocrypha*. I think you may find there's an intriguing little puzzle contained in its history."

The Veterans

LATELY, SHERIFF DIRKS' SMALL DEPARTMENT SEEMED to have had more than its fair share of murder cases. As to the latest one, the investigation had gotten off to a slow start, but now it was wrapping up nicely.

Then why did Dirks have these nagging doubts?

As had become his habit, the sheriff took his doubts to the elderly clergyman who had given him good advice in the past. This Catholic priest had given equally good advice to many people over the years, but for Sheriff Dirks, Father Brown's insights into criminal behavior and motives had been exceptionally helpful.

The murder case began when a resident of an upscale neighborhood north of the town center put in an emergency call to the sheriff's department. A man named Stern had dialed 9-1-1 from his bedroom at two in the morning. He said he had just caught sight of intruders sneaking around his house.

"In one way we caught a break," Dirks said. "Deputy Mill was driving by the house when Stern's call came in. Mill was supposed to be downtown, but he said things were so quiet he decided to cruise the residential area. When the call came, Mill didn't wait for backup as he certainly should have. He entered right away. He didn't find any intruders, but he found Stern's dead body in the bedroom no more than minutes after the man had been attacked. Somebody had bashed in the guy's head with a baseball bat. Also, a good deal of jewelry and things turned up missing. The killer, it seems, was there for the loot."

Dirks went on to explain that he had no leads at all until about a week after the murder when a man walked into the District Attorney's office and said he wanted to make a deal. He said two friends of his had been the ones Stern had seen sneaking around in his house. He said these friends would confess to the burglary but not to hitting anyone with a ball bat.

"Before long," Dirks said, "we had roped in three of this guy's pals. They were old army buddies from the Korean War days, and after the war each one of them had tried to start a business. They all four went broke. They've got okay jobs now, but I guess they wanted a little more in the kitty than what they were getting out of their wages.

"One of the vets works for a bug exterminator, so he's inside a lot of homes; he picks the best targets for theft. Another of them installs home security systems—burglar alarms—a useful trade with skills a burglar would find helpful, obviously. Another one of them tried opening a jewelry store years ago, but the business failed. Now he's repairing jewelry in the backroom at Bosco's, and lately he's been running a small we-buy-and-sell-gold business on the side. Well, he sells it, but he only pretends to buy it. He gets his gold out of other people's houses. The fourth vet works the front counter at the post office, which is another useful line of work. He knew people were planning to go out of town when they handed in their 'Stop Mail Delivery' forms."

Dirks noticed the blank look on Father Brown's face. "Well, Father," he said, "People don't want mail or other deliveries piling up at the front door. It signals that they're away."

"I see," said Father Brown.

"Anyway, these birds were very surprised to find Stern at home. Turns out the poor guy got busy at work and had to send his wife and kids off on vacation without him. His widow says he was going to join them in a day or two. That's how the burglars got tripped up. They never intended to break into a house when one of the owners was at home."

"How many of those veterans were in the Stern house, Sheriff?" Father Brown asked.

"Two," Dirks said. "And get this. They say they realized somebody was at home when they heard voices coming from the bedroom. They both swear it was a man and a woman. They were about finished gathering loot, so they started to leave by the front door. They changed their minds when they saw the squad car parked in front of the house, and so they beat it out through the patio in back."

"Do you believe their story about a woman being there?" Father Brown asked.

"Not really," Dirks said. "We can't find any rumors of a woman involved with Stern. We think the vets invented her just to take the heat off. You know, to put some other suspect at the scene."

Father Brown looked at the palm of his hand for a few moments. Then he said, "I'm afraid my sympathies tend to lie with soldiers who have risked their lives for their country. Not just my own English soldiers, but soldiers of any country—a country they love and call home and fight to defend. But let's talk about this again, Sheriff, after you've interviewed Deputy Mill's wife."

"Nancy?" Dirks asked. "Why?"

"You'll see, I think," Father Brown replied, and he showed Dirks to the door with a friendly goodbye and nothing more.

A week later, Sheriff Dirks found himself once again congratulating Father Brown. "Now will you show me your crystal ball?" he asked.

"Such foolishness," the priest said with a chuckle. "It's merely common sense. You see, there was one part of your story that did not hang together—at least based on the facts you gave me—and that was Officer Mill's behavior. He had no business being in that neighborhood; and the way you explained it, he didn't seem to be patrolling, if that's the word. He seemed to be watching that specific house. Watching for what?"

"But I still don't…"

"Look at it from this direction," Father Brown continued, waving a hand. "Mill was looking for one of two things—burglary or infidelity, but how could it have been burglary? He didn't say he saw anything suspicious or that somebody warned him about a possible criminal housebreaking. No, it was much more likely he was interested in something else that was going on in that particular house on that particular street."

"Yeah," Dirks said. "Nancy spilled it all. She was with Stern that night. Stern thought he could slip her out before we got there. He was flabbergasted when Deputy Mill was in his face just seconds after he made his phone call to our headquarters. Mill told his wife to beat it home before the house was overrun with cops, and so she left the two men alone together. You know what happened next.

"It's a tough thing to accept when a policeman turns criminal, but maybe it was temporary insanity—a jealous rage. Our investigation got confused because of the burglary. Well, anyway, now that Deputy Mill has confessed, I'm in your debt again. Is there any possible way I can repay you, Father Brown?"

"Those four burglars served their country," the priest said, "and they have had precious little reward for their pains. What they did—that burglary business—was wrong, but will you try to get the prosecutors to consider their former service and grant them as much leniency as your laws permit?"

"Okay," Dirks said. "I can do that."

And he did.

The Sheriff Bluffs

CLEM SMITH IS WEALTHY. HE SPENDS HIS WINTERS IN Florida and his summers in the Midwest at his sumptuous beach house on the shores of a small lake in Bardo County. From his impressive third-floor balcony, or so Smith's houseguests testify, the view of the setting sun is truly spectacular.

The great love of Mr. Smith, aside from money, is the game of chess. Any serious player visiting the area is likely to find himself invited to one of Smith's monthly "chess dinners." The lucky guest will visit Smith's great balcony, furnished with tables and all the equipment of the game; and, at his host's own table, he will see Smith's celebrated golden-jeweled chess pieces. The gold and jewels and the exquisite workmanship make the set valuable beyond price.

The local sheriff, whose name is Dirks, is a reliable if unimaginative club player, and he was happy to accept his third invitation to a Smith chess evening. He arrived early and was paired against a stockbroker from Chicago named Ted, a superior player. Dirks was soon found himself locked into a cramped and indefensible position. He quickly resigned.

"What happens next?" Ted asked. Dirks explained that they could watch the other games or absorb the view from the balcony's balustrade.

"After dinner," Dirks said, "we'll come back out here for brandy, cigars, and speed chess." To Ted this sounded like great fun.

They stopped to observe the opening moves of a game between Sam, a local player, and a visiting Catholic priest from Cleveland. The two kings' pawns faced each other in the center of the board. On his second move, Sam, playing white, threatened with a knight; and, as expected, the clergyman defended with a knight. Sam then played his king's bishop, and the priest abruptly moved his knight a second time, crashing it into the center and leaving his pawn undefended.

After the pawn was gobbled up, Dirks and his new friend Ted watched as the priest brought his queen into play. Then they walked to the balustrade to have a chat, which they agreed to continue over their after-dinner drinks.

At the dinner, Dirks was seated across from the priest, who was wearing fashionable resort wear rather than a Roman collar. Earlier, Dirks had noticed that the man was sporting an expensive wristwatch and a large gold finger ring with an over-sized diamond. Dirks began listening to him.

"No, no," he was saying, "Hell is just a symbol for evil. So is the devil, or Satan. Satan is not a being who exists as we do. These things are real enough, in their way, but not real in the sense you mean."

At that point, Dirks lost the thread of the conversation. Dinner was soon over, and it was time for a little rough and tumble speed chess. As he wandered out onto the balcony, he was suddenly confronted by his host, who seemed very upset.

"Sheriff," Smith wailed, "somebody has stolen my chess-men!" It was true. The board was bare. The precious gold figures had disappeared.

It took Dirks only a few minutes to find the nylon rope tied to a baluster and dangling down to the beach below. One of the guests must have attached the rope earlier in the evening to set up an accomplice who would climb up during dinner and pinch the gold figures. The sheriff warned the guests not to leave the county, and then he sent them home—except for one man whom he especially wanted to question.

The next day, Dirks paid a call on his elderly friend, Father Brown. He was sure he would enjoy telling the priest about his triumph over the priest who was a thief.

"It's all wrapped up," he said. "That priest was as phony as a three-ring sideshow."

"A counterfeit priest," Father Brown said. "How interesting! What led you to suspect him?"

"The guy was supposed to be a chess player," Dirks said. He described the opening moves of the game he and the stockbro-ker had watched on Clem Smith's balcony. "That third move was the giveaway, Father. No grammar school kid would make that blunder. It got me thinking."

"Thinking about what?" Father Brown asked.

Dirks said he had noticed the priest's expensive clothes and jewelry. "If he's really a Catholic priest," he argued, "where's the vow of poverty?"

Father Brown's face wore a deep scowl. "Anything else, Sheriff?" he asked.

"Just this," Dirks said. "I heard him say at dinner that Satan and Hell aren't real. I'm not religious myself, as you know per-fectly well, Father, but you and all the other Catholics I know really do believe in things like that."

Father Brown seemed lost in thought. At last he said, "I'm terribly sorry, Sheriff, but I do think you have arrested the wrong man."

"Why?" Dirks asked.

Father Brown patiently explained that parish priests don't make a vow of poverty. "Perhaps the expensive timepiece was a Christmas present from his mother," he suggested. "It's conceivable that the diamond ring had belonged to his own father, but, Sheriff, it is not unusual for a parish priest to have money."

"Oh," Dirks said.

"And his ideas about Hell are not Catholic," Father Brown continued, "and I do not endorse them; but I have known priests who think that way. They tell me their ideas are in the *spirit* if not the *letter* of Church doctrine."

"I see," Dirks said, quietly.

"And his third move was not a blunder. I don't know much about chess, but I can tell you that this priest was playing an old trick opening called the 'Shilling Gambit.' It was the stock in trade of Joseph Blackburne, a chess expert and a man I actually met once back in England. He made a living playing the gambit against gullible amateurs for a shilling a game. His were always quick games—a quick win if his gambit were successful, which it almost always was, and a quick loss on the rare occasions when it failed. Didn't the priest explain all this to you?"

"Well," Dirks said, a bit guiltily, "I knew my inferences weren't solid evidence, Father, so I decided to bluff. I told him a witness had seen him set the rope on the balcony."

"That must have been a frightening thing for an innocent man to hear," Father Brown said.

"Are you kidding?" Dirks said. "The bluff worked. The guy went for a deal. He's a con artist, and that priest act was just part of his game. Anyhow, the fancy chess pieces are back on Smith's balcony where they belong."

Father Brown stared at him in astonishment. Finally, he said, "I see now that your inferences were sound after all."

"I see now they were worthless," Dirks said sheepishly. "I had the right man for all the wrong reasons. I was very, very lucky. But I did learn something I never knew before."

"Do you mean," Father Brown asked, "you learned that in chess you can't always tell a gambit from a blunder?"

"There is that," Dirks said. "But what I meant was I learned you can't always tell a Catholic priest from an atheist."

"Oh," said Father Brown.

The Feud

Vic Pierce and Ken Larson were neighbors with homes on a small lake in Bardo County, and the feud between them had been approaching the boiling point for some months. Vic valued privacy and did not like Ken's habit of trespassing on his beach. For his part, Ken thought of the beach frontage around the lake as a sort of commons to be shared by all the neighbors.

Things came to a head when Vic erected two ugly barrier fences complete with "Private Property—Keep Out!" signs. Ken quickly called Sheriff Dirks to protest, but the sheriff suggested he take his grievance to the homeowners' association.

To Ken's surprise and vexation, the board members sided with Vic.

"We know the fences are ugly," said John Sayers, the association's president, "but you caused the problem in the first place, Ken. If you'll give us your word you'll not step foot on Vic's private property, I think we can persuade him to take the fences down."

Ken burst out of the meeting so angry that he didn't even notice the even angrier rainstorm beating down on him.

Before noon the next day, Vic Pierce was dead.

The case was an exasperating one for the sheriff. Finally, he decided to call on his elderly friend, a Catholic priest whose insights into crimes and criminals had often come to his rescue. After hanging his raincoat on the coat rack, he happily accepted the steaming mug of hot chocolate that Mrs. James the rectory's housekeeper offered.

"Will this rain ever stop?" he asked wearily.

"The newspaper promises sunshine tomorrow," Father Brown answered, "but you have something else on your mind, Sheriff. What have you come to tell me?"

"There were no tracks," said Dirks.

"Maybe you should start from the beginning," Father Brown suggested.

"Yeah, okay," Dirks said, and went on to explain his problem. After describing the feud between the two neighbors, he told Father Brown that the morning after the homeowners' board meeting, Vic's wife Doris had glanced out of a window that overlooked the beach, and she spotted Ken Larson in the act of vandalizing Vic's boat.

"It was a large dory or dinghy propped up on struts for repairs. Doris called the sheriff's department to say she had seen Ken out there in a wetsuit, and that he pushed on the boat until it fell off its props. She said the boat landed heavily on the beach and was probably damaged. Ken then just walked away, according to Doris."

Dirks said that his department was extra busy that morning, and so it was more than three hours before he could send a deputy to look the situation over. "I didn't see any special urgency," Dirks said, "and neither did Doris. She didn't even bother to go out to inspect the boat."

The deputy found the boat lying on its side in the sand about twenty feet from the water's edge. Then he noticed something else halfway between the boat and the water. Vic's body lay sprawled on the sand, the shaft of a small harpoon sticking up from his chest. He had been speared by someone looming over him as he lay there sleeping.

"I can place Ken Larson at the scene at the approximate time of Vic's death," Dirks continued, "and since he was an avid spear fisherman, I can show he had the weapon. It will be easy enough to establish the motive. So, it's an open and shut case—except for one thing."

"There were no tracks," said Father Brown, smiling as he remembered how their conversation had begun.

"There were no prints or tracks between the body and the lake," Dirks said, "or between the body and the boat, or forty feet to either side. Waves could not have erased any prints because the breeze that morning wasn't anything like the sort of gale you'd need to drive waves twenty feet up the beach. One of my deputies thinks the harpoon was shot out of a low flying hot-air balloon. Phooey. I told him *he's* a hot-air balloon."

"You can't convict Larson on the evidence you have?" Father Brown asked.

"Not in a jury trial," said Dirks. "The defense would focus on the impossibility of Ken going to and from the body without leaving tracks. We could convict if we had a plausible guess as to why there weren't tracks. But we have nothing."

"There's been a terrific amount of rain around here lately."

"Yeah, Father, we've had record-breaking rainfalls," said Dirks, "but on that morning we had clear skies from dawn until mid-afternoon. There wasn't any rain to wash away footprints."

"What about wind?"

"No," said Dirks. "The sun baked and dried everything on the beach including the sand, but an inch or two below the surface the sand was still saturated with rain water. The surface might have shifted a bit in that light breeze, but not enough to erase footprints."

"Might not Ken have been outfitted with those funny fin things that, if I'm not mistaken, underwater swimmers wear on their feet?" the priest asked.

"If he did, the footprints might not have been as deep," Dirks said, "but he'd still leave a track."

Father Brown considered this. "Can you ask Doris how long Vic had been working on his boat-repair hobby?" he asked.

"I don't have to," Dirks said. "I knew Vic. He took the boat out of the water in early spring, and he hasn't done a lick of work on it since. The truth is he'd rather sleep in the sun. We used to kid him about it. But, it doesn't matter now that he's joined the ranks of the dearly departed."

"It matters a great deal," said Father Brown. "It might win your case."

"Well then, Father, you have my undivided attention," said Dirks.

"I don't think the murder was planned," Father Brown said. "I see Ken doing some underwater spear fishing, if that's what it's called, and then spotting Vic napping in the sun. I can picture him walking out of the water and standing over his enemy. And then, in a sudden fit of rage—which was part of his character from what you've told me—I can see how he might have put a final end to that foolish feud of theirs. And last, in my imagination at least, there he is walking the few more steps up the beach to tip over Vic's boat as a final act of hatred and contempt."

"Well of course you think that," said Dirks. "I do, too."

"Sheriff, you said Vic's boat had been propped up there on the beach since early spring. With that last storm, I think I read that we have had almost three feet of rain. I wonder if Vic's boat wasn't—"

"—full of water," Dirks said, snapping his fingers. "And that's the ticket. All that water flowing down the beach might—"

"It very well might," said Father Brown.

Dirks finished his hot chocolate and reached for his hat and raincoat, rushing his thanks and his farewell. He was a man in a hurry.

As usual, events proved Father Brown's guess to have been precisely right. When Ken finally confessed, he admitted that he was still in a rage when he toppled Vic's boat. He was surprised and overjoyed when he saw the water gush down the beach, believing it had washed away his guilt.

The Blackmailer

THE REASON MARK BENTLEY AND HIS BROTHER RALPH so often changed residences and moved from town to town had to do with the special way in which they earned their money. The men were making quite a good living out of both burglaries and blackmail. In fact Ralph's burglaries often provided Mark with material he could use in his blackmailing schemes. Just recently, as an example of this, they had learned that one of the most prominent businessmen in their latest community had been keeping two sets of books, one at work and the other at home.

A parlor maid opened the door and ushered Mark into a large study. She could not help but notice that he was an imposing looking man. Mark was thin and tall—six-foot-six, bald as an egg, and his shiny white scalp contrasted strongly with his jet black mustache and matching Van Dyke beard. The man he was visiting, Clayton Farmer, was older—in his fifties compared to Mark's thirty-five years—and he had the tired look of someone who is overworked and over worried. He was seated behind a desk apparently studying the papers that were stacked in front of him. He gestured for Mark to sit in one of the chairs facing his desk. Mark sat and, without any introductory remarks or other formalities, he drew a paper out of his breast pocket and pushed it across the desk. Farmer glanced at it, and looked up with alarm.

"It's very simple," Mark said. "You give me a cashier's check for $10,000, and I give you back your journal. If you decide not to cooperate with me, I will see to it that these materials find their way into the hands of the proper authorities. I mean the authorities who disapprove of embezzlers who keep two sets of books."

Farmer stared at his visitor in silence for a full minute by the clock. Then he cleared his throat and said the following: "Mr. Bentley, I am not going to travel down that road with you. You want $10,000 now. How much will you want next month? How many copies of that ledger have you made? No, I'll take my chances with the courts and my ability to hire and pay for the best legal defense team money can buy."

Mark said nothing. He stood and walked to the wall behind Farmer's desk and stared out the window.

"One more thing, Mr. Bentley," Farmer said. "If you go through with your threat, I do believe these 'authorities,' as you call them, will be interested in this photocopy you've provided for me. Your fingerprints are all over it. Blackmail is a felony too, and so is burglary; and I think the penalties are more severe for those crimes than for embezzlement, which is merely about bookkeeping."

Mark wheeled around and leaned on Farmer's desk. "I have the answer for that," he said, and in one swift motion he picked up a metal letter opener and drove it into the seated man's windpipe. Farmer fell forward, his head and chest coming to rest on the desk. Mark watched as his victim choked out his last breath. Then he calmly emptied the contents of Farmer's wastepaper basket and retrieved its plastic liner. He pulled the bloody letter opener from his victim's throat and dropped it into the liner and tied a knot in the open end. This package disappeared into one of his pockets. He retrieved the copy of the journal page. As he left the study, Mark told a second maid that he would let himself out, and he hurried away.

◼   ◼   ◼

In the early stages of his investigation, Sheriff Dirks had thought he had an open and shut case. Two witnesses, the parlor maids, described the same man, a man with a very distinctive appearance. Then the two had independently picked Mark Bentley out of a lineup, swearing in no uncertain terms that he was the one who had visited Farmer in his study.

Bentley claimed to have an alibi. He swore that at the time the crime had been committed, he had been dining in a local restaurant. Unfortunately for the sheriff's case, a dozen witnesses were found who were ready to swear that Bentley had been in their sight in this restaurant from well before the time of the murder until well after. The parlor maids obviously had been badly mistaken about the time of Bentley's visit.

"Why me?" the disgusted sheriff asked Father Brown after he had explained the circumstances of the case. "Why do I keep coming up with these doozies?"

Father Brown had listened without commenting to the sheriff's description of the facts surrounding the Farmer murder. Then he sat and silently stroked his chin. After a very long moment he said, "Sheriff, when I was a much younger man I used to enjoy reading murder mysteries."

"I thought you never read anything but Shakespeare and Dickens."

Father Brown laughed. "Why, Sheriff," he said, "you've often seen me assessing the literary merits of the *Bardo County Sentinel*. But about those detective stories…"

Dirks waved his hand impatiently. "I never had time for that stuff," he said. "Anyone making a living enforcing the law is not going to enjoy spending his spare time reading about his job. It would be like going back to work when you could be playing canasta or watching television."

"Oh, I understand that perfectly well," Father Brown replied. "Those tales were not about what real murderers and real sheriffs do in this world. They were more in the manner of puzzles or riddles, in which the author was playing a game of wits with his readers."

"With all due respect," said Dirks, "I can't see how a discussion of fun and games is going to be helpful in an actual real-life murder investigation."

"Then let me tell you something about those stories that might suggest something helpful."

"Okay," said the sheriff, settling back in his chair.

"Now, when I was reading detective stories of the puzzle kind, my pet peeve had to do with authors who did not play the game with fairness. I mean they would suddenly at the end of the story introduce something to explain the mysterious crime, but it too often was something for which they had not prepared their readers. A suspect, let us say, could not have visited the scene of the crime because he was barred from entry by a high fence. Then, on the very last page, the readers are informed, and for the first time, that this suspect had once been a vaulting champion."

"But what does this have to do with anything?" Dirks asked with a vigorous shake of his head.

"Perhaps this," Father Brown said. "One of the favorite devices used by this class of authors was to clear up a mystery by introducing a twin brother in the final scene to explain how witnesses could have seen a suspect in two places at once."

"Could we get back to this case that I'm—" Dirks stopped and stared at Father Brown. Then he clapped both hands to his forehead and said, "Father, I would save us both a lot of time if I could just learn to shut up and listen."

Once they knew what they were looking for, it did not take long for Sheriff Dirks and his deputies to track down and arrest the Bentley twins. A search warrant provided all the evidence needed for two convictions and two very long prison terms.

An After-Dinner Drink

SHERIFF DIRKS GENERALLY FELT SOME COMPASSION FOR even the worst of the criminals he pursued and arrested in the line of duty. A central exhibit in his sympathetic approach was the case of one Carl Defoe.

This man was as convivial a host as any in Bardo county, which had always been known as a fairly friendly neighborhood in a fairly congenial region of the Midwest. Carl's summer home—the gentleman wintered in Florida—was an old-fashioned country mansion, comfortably appointed and well staffed, and his friends looked forward eagerly to his invitations. Yet Carl, now in his seventies, had come to prefer small and informal get-togethers with his relatives.

He had never married, but he was as close to his late brother's three children as any father could be. On the weekend in question, he was delighted to entertain Sarah and her physician husband Doctor James Moore, Bill and his wife Sally, and Ron, who was single. The group enjoyed their frequent weekends together, playing cards, enjoying leisurely meals and cocktails, discussing the arts in a friendly spirit, and permitting themselves to be entertained by Ron's endless stories and jokes.

On Friday night, Carl had retired early to attend to a pressing financial problem. It had to be settled, he said, before he could properly enjoy the weekend. Though he had asked not to be disturbed, Sarah decided to look in on him later, and her scream brought the rest of the party on the run. They found Carl sprawled on the floor by his desk on which rested a number of documents, an open bottle of Amaretto, and a nearly empty glass tumbler. After a brief examination, Doctor Moore pronounced the man dead.

"I'm not sure," he told them, "but I think he may have been poisoned."

They all agreed that their uncle must have been the victim of a bizarre sort of accident. They also agreed that the police might not see it that way. Ron immediately took charge and wisely ordered them not to touch anything in the room. He wanted to be able to promise the police that no one had tampered with the scene of the accident or, if the police so judged it, the scene of the crime. Next, he asked Bill to phone the sheriff, and he called for the group to reassemble in the drawing room and wait there.

"They're all telling the same story," Sheriff Dirks was saying. The sheriff was enjoying some bits of cheese and a glass of wine in the rectory of St. Dominic's as he outlined the facts surrounding Defoe's perplexing death for his friend Father Brown.

"Maybe they're all telling the same lie," the priest said with a smile.

"I considered that," Dirks said, "but the old servant Kerns is too simple a man for a conspiracy. He wouldn't be able to keep a concocted story straight under intense questioning, and they all swear no one left the drawing room the entire time. The stairway was in plain sight, and there are three or four steps that creak so badly you could not sneak up the stairs unnoticed."

The sheriff then explained that Carl Defoe had died of cyanide poisoning. The medical examiner assumed that the poison had been mixed with the Amaretto as a flavor mask, because both substances have a strong almond flavor. To everyone's surprise, the partially empty bottle and the nearly empty tumbler on Defoe's desk contained pure Amaretto without a trace of anything poisonous.

"It was Defoe's favorite after-dinner beverage," Dirks explained. "He drank it in great gulps without benefit of ice or water, but he never kept a supply of any kind of liquor in his room. That old servant swears such a thing would go against the man's customs and habits of a lifetime. Kerns was the last one in Defoe's room and the last to see him alive, and he says he is certain there was no bottle on the man's desk, because if a bottle had been there he would have seen it, and he would have been so surprised he would certainly have remembered it. When Kerns went downstairs to the drawing room, his employer was still alive according to the time of death worked out by the medical examiner. So we can't pin anything on Kerns.

"The five guests and the old servant stayed together in the drawing room for the next two hours," Dirks continued. "Kerns insisted on staying to see to their needs, and no one left, not even to visit the powder room. Oh, and the only route to and from Defoe's room is that staircase. There's no back stairway as you might expect."

"Were Mr. Defoe's fingerprints on the bottle?"

"No," said Dirks, "there were no prints on it."

"Do you mean the prints were smudged?" Father Brown asked.

"No," said Dirks. "There were no prints on it at all. Say, Father, what are you getting at? What am I missing?"

"In so far as I can judge from this distance, Sheriff," Father Brown said, "you've done very thorough work. You know where everyone was and what they were doing just before Defoe's death—with one exception."

"What?" Dirks said, coming out of his chair. "What exception?"

"Carl Defoe's own movements before his death," Father Brown replied. "Oh, please don't look so bewildered, Sheriff. There is only one way to read the facts as you have related them, and I'm prepared to read them for you."

Dirks sat down. "Please go ahead," he said.

"By your account, Mr. Defoe's niece and nephews were his next of kin, and he was fond of them; I am surmising that they were his heirs. Every soul has its secrets, of course, but I suspect that Ron's friendly cordiality was nothing more than a pose. His only genuine interest was his share in the estate.

"Knowing his uncle's fondness for his almond-flavored drink, he probably had the almond-flavored poison with him on previous visits—waiting for his chance; but this time, when Defoe dispensed with his usual brandy at dinner's end, Ron saw it as the opportunity he was waiting for. He told his uncle that there was a full bottle of Amaretto down the hallway on the desk in his own room, and that his uncle was welcome to help himself to it if he felt thirsty. Of course he had already laced its contents with cyanide. After an hour or so of financial work, I believe Mr. Defoe decided he missed his customary drink—the power of suggestion, I believe it is called—and went off to take advantage of his nephew's offer. As the nephew had probably surmised he would, Defoe brought the bottle back to his room where he planned to continue his work.

"Ron knew the autopsy would show Carl had been drinking Amaretto as well as cyanide. So, after he ordered his cousins downstairs, he had just enough time to switch bottles and tumblers, wipe off his prints, and hide the contaminated evidence, thus creating a mystery. The rest you know."

Dirks considered this for a minute or two. "How can I prove it?" he asked.

"I don't know," Father Brown said, simply enough.

Proofs were unnecessary. When Dirks suddenly confronted Ron with Father Brown's conjectures, the man was shocked into admitting his guilt. "I was tired of waiting around for the old buzzard to drop dead," he said by way of an excuse. "I need money."

Sheriff Dirks generally felt some compassion for even the worst of the criminals it was his duty to pursue and arrest.

Not this time.

Corpus Delicti

SHERIFF DIRKS WAS SITTING AT THE KITCHEN TABLE enjoying an omelet and a cup of hot coffee. His companion was enjoying hot tea. "Don't tell Marie," Dirks said, "but your housekeeper makes the best omelets in Bardo County."

"Your secret is safe with us," said Father Brown. "Our lips are sealed in the name of domestic tranquility. But tell me about this new investigation that has you so troubled."

"This case is as frustrating as anything I can remember, Father Brown. And it's not something you can help me with because we know darned well who committed the crime. There's no mystery for you to solve in that part of the case. I almost wish that *was* the problem."

"What is the problem, then?" the priest asked.

"The problem is we can't find the body. Even though we're sure this man was murdered, we can't prove there was a murder without the body. The courts call it *corpus delicti*. It means that the first thing law enforcement has to do is establish that there actually was a crime. Until that's in hand, nothing else matters."

"Your problem seems extremely interesting on the face of it," said Father Brown. "You say you know the victim was murdered, but you haven't said how you know it."

"Well, you'll see when I play this recording," Dirks said, pointing to the portable tape recorder he had placed on the table. "We have the killer on tape admitting that he buried the body somewhere under the sand of a beach. But I should begin at the beginning, and not in the middle of things."

Dirks then related how Max Osborn, a mechanic at Gerber's Ford-Mercury, had failed to show up for work. He had never before missed a day on the job, and his boss, Jerry Gerber, was worried. When he phoned Osborn's home there was no answer; he sent a teenager employee to Osborn's home. The boy returned with the information that he couldn't get anyone to answer the doorbell.

"This Osborn guy hasn't been seen from that day to this," the sheriff said. "Now, Father, I know you're going to say that it might be just a missing-persons case, so first let me give you some facts that point to murder."

"Of course, Sheriff," the priest said. "I'm sure there is much more to this than you've had time to explain."

"You've got that right," Dirks said. "First of all, there was a pool of blood on the floor in Osborn's front entry. His wife—her name's Hannah—she works for Tupperware, and she was in Atlantic City at the time. She was at a Tupperware convention, and get this, Father, they call these shindigs 'Jubilees.'"

"I'm afraid I don't know what manner of thing Tupperware might be," the priest admitted, "but if the word *jubilee* still means anything, Mrs. Osborn and her associates were celebrating a year of emancipation and restoration."

"I kind of doubt that, Father," Dirks said. "But anyhow, I assigned a deputy to try to reach her by phone and, if that didn't work out, I told him to enlist the help of the Atlantic City police. When we finally did get to her, she came back here right away, but of course she had an airtight alibi. She can prove she was hundreds of miles away when her hubby disappeared."

Father Brown simply nodded, and Dirks then explained how they had learned from the neighbors that Hannah Osborn had a boyfriend, a man named Herman Sterns; although, apparently, Max Osborn had not an inkling of what his wife was doing behind his back.

Early in the investigation, the sheriff said, he had persuaded Judge Lunt to authorize a wiretap of the phone in the man's apartment. "We got lucky, because one of the first calls we recorded was from Hannah Osborn from Atlantic City. Now let me play the key part for you, because the rest of the tape won't interest you. In fact, Father, you might find it offensive. But anyhow, here's the typed transcript of what *will* interest you, so you can read and listen at the same time."

Dirks handed Father Brown a small sheet of paper and then pushed a lever on the tape recorder. A woman's voice said (and the transcript read), *"Did you finish the project?"*

Then a man's voice said, *"Everything's done. It's perfect. Not a hitch. The, um, package is in the beach, very far down where it will never be found."*

"It seems a rum way of putting it," Father Brown said, fingering the piece of paper.

"How do you mean?"

"I would have expected him to say 'The package is *buried* in the beach.'"

"Okay," Dirks said, "but if we can put the grammar lesson aside and get back to the case, I'll tell you something about the geography. The Osbornes live on a street where the rear of the residential properties borders on a big woods. If you walk west through the woods for about three miles, you come to a small lake with a sandy beach all the way around it. We've talked about this beach before, Father, if you remember that case where a man was murdered while he was napping on the sand."

"Yes, I remember. It was the year we had the rainiest summer on record."

The sheriff then explained that he and his men had searched the beach with metal detectors and with a pair of bloodhounds. Finally they took thin metal rods and systematically probed every inch of the beach hoping to find the buried body. They found any amount of buried litter, but no body.

"And that's where the investigation stands. It stands at a standstill."

Father Brown stared for a moment at his empty teacup, and Sheriff Dirks held his breath. Then the priest said, "I have an idea of sorts for you, Sheriff, but don't be impatient with me if I tell you the idea comes from a murder mystery I once read."

"I've learned my lesson, Father. Tell me the idea."

"First give me your opinion about how old this stand of trees is that you said lies between the Osborn home and the lake."

"It's plenty old. It was old when I was a kid."

"Many years ago—enough years ago that I can't count them—I read a short story published in England about a killer who hid the corpse of his victim in the hollow of a huge tree."

The sheriff stood up and shook his head with some impatience. "The recording of that phone call," he said, "tells us the body—he called it 'the package'—is buried deep in the beach."

"Yes, I know," Father Brown replied, "and I see in this transcript you have spelled out the word b-e-a-c-h. You might as well have spelled it b-e-e-c-h. You see, Sheriff, the tree in that old story was a giant beech tree, and I am wondering why your Mr. Sterns would carry a heavy burden for three miles for a burial in a beach where he could easily be observed—especially if there were a hiding place closer to hand." And seeing that the sheriff's mouth was gaping open, he added, "I can't promise you that my idea is the right one, but you might want to put it to the test."

It took the help of a dozen volunteer searchers, but Max Osborn's body and his pistol were found wrapped together in a bloody throw rug and hidden in a large fissure in a giant-sized beech tree not more than two hundred paces from the Osborn home. The pistol proved to be the murder weapon, and a few days later the sheriff had the confessions of both Hannah Osborn and Herman Sterns.

Finding Debbie

FATHER BROWN SOMETIMES REMEMBERED THE CASE with sadness, sometimes with joy, but never without an amused chuckle, for he could not deny the affair was tinged with a hint of the ridiculous. His involvement in the crime began with a visit from his friend Sheriff Dirks. The sheriff often described his investigations to Father Brown, and the old priest had been singularly helpful to him in the past. Although now in his nineties, Father Brown still had an agile mind, and his knowledge of the human heart was profound.

"This thing we're working on might be right up your alley," Dirks said as he gratefully accepted the glass of diet cola offered by Mrs. James, the rectory's friendly housekeeper. "It's full of contradictions, so I expect you'll untangle it for me in a few seconds."

"What are the details, Sheriff?" Father Brown said, ignoring the compliment.

"It's a hit and run accident," Dirks said. "The pedestrian who was run down died almost immediately. Two passersby tried to help, and one of them phoned us as soon as he could, but the ambulance was too late to save the poor old guy."

Father Brown smiled at the Americanism. "Who was this poor old *guy*?" he asked.

"Name was Earl Jenness," Dirks replied. "Oh, I am sorry, Father Brown. Judging by the look on your face, you must have known him."

Father Brown sat in silence for a few moments, his eyes shut. Then he crossed himself and turned his gaze on the sheriff. "Yes," he said, "we were friends. He used to give lectures on literature at the Fair Lane Arts Teachers' College, and we often discussed Shakespeare and Charles Dickens. I certainly will miss him. He was old enough that we could talk together of things the world has forgotten."

"I really am sorry," said Dirks.

"He was once a seminarian," Father Brown said, and seeing the sheriff's blank expression, he added, "he was studying to be a priest, but in the end he decided he did not have the true calling."

"Does that have to do with things the world has forgotten?" Dirks asked.

"Well, yes. We were an ocean apart, but his experiences and training were quite similar to my own. Earl was a devoted and helpful parishioner here. Father Bell will miss him every bit as much as I will. But please tell me more about it."

"Right," said Dirks. "First we canvassed the neighborhood looking for possible witnesses. Nobody saw the accident, but one housewife described a panel truck she saw racing away from the scene at about the right time. She wasn't sure of the make, but she said it had a big tiger painted on the side. We found the truck, and the housewife was prepared to swear it was the one she saw. There aren't many trucks around here painted with that sort of tiger—or any sort of tiger, for that matter."

"And the driver denies he was the one who collided with Earl?"

"Sure he does. And we couldn't see any dents or signs of an accident on the truck."

"Aren't there scientific people," Father Brown asked, "who could study the vehicle with microscopes for invisible clues and the like?"

"We came up empty in that department, too," said Dirks. "The forensics gal couldn't find anything. We did learn that the suspect had been to the car wash after the time of the accident, and that might have something to do with the lack of trace evidence."

At this point the housekeeper interrupted to offer Father Brown a cup of tea and Dirks a second glass of cola, which both men gratefully accepted.

"Anyway," the sheriff continued, "we can't press the guy too hard because we have other evidence pointing in a different direction. If he did it, we can break him down, but we doubt he did."

"Oh?" said Father Brown in surprise. He had been thinking the solution to the case would prove to be unusually simple and straightforward.

"The passerby who stayed at the scene said the dying man had tried to tell him something. Your friend was in bad shape, with broken ribs and his lungs smashed in. He could hardly breathe let alone talk, and most of what he said was gibberish. At least that's the testimony."

"But not everything was gibberish?"

"He said he thought the man was trying to tell him the car that hit him was a Fiat," Dirks said, "and that he knew the driver. He mentioned the name 'Debbie' twice. In fact, the last word he uttered was very distinctly 'Debbie.' We've been searching for a Debbie who drives a Fiat."

Father Brown looked puzzled. "Don't tell me there's a motorcar named 'Fiat,'" he said. "Great heavens!"

The sheriff glanced at his watch. "Oh, no!" he said. "I'm late for dinner again, and Marie is going to kill me." And grabbing his hat while offering apologies for his abruptness, Sheriff Dirks headed for the door.

"I can tell you one thing," Father Brown said. "You can forget about Debbie and concentrate on the man with the tiger."

This stopped Dirks in his tracks. He swiveled around to face the priest. "How do you know that?"

"If I tell you now," Father Brown answered, "you'll be even later for dinner, and I'll be in trouble with Mrs. Dirks. We can't have that, so you'll just have to trust me."

"You've never steered me wrong, Father," Dirks said, and he was gone.

■   ■   ■

On the following evening, the sheriff was all smiles as Mrs. James ushered him back into the sitting room where Father Brown was busy studying a small black leather-bound book.

"Am I interrupting you, Father?" Dirks said.

"Yes," the priest said with simple honesty, "but I can finish this later."

"You were right," Dirks said. "We cracked that guy with the panel truck once we knew there was no Debbie in the case. He wasn't so tough, as it turned out. But I'm here to find out how you knew."

"Or rather *what* I knew," Father Brown said. "I didn't think Earl Jenness would be able to say which kind of motorcar had struck him down. It's more likely he never even saw the truck coming."

"Well that's a good point," Dirks conceded.

"But much more important," Father Brown continued, "was the idea that Earl would spend his last breath attempting to identify a criminal." To the inquiring look Dirks gave him, Father Brown replied, "I dare say Earl Jenness would have spent his last breath in prayer."

"There's a 'Debbie' prayer?" Dirks asked in all seriousness.

"We priests of a certain age were trained to recite the Lord's Prayer in Latin. Surely in his pain Jim's voice must have been twisted, distorting his pronunciation. The relevant words of the prayer are *fiat*—'let it be done,' *debita*—'debts,' and *debitoribus* —'debtors.' He died before he finished pronouncing that last word. He said '*debi*'..."

Sheriff Dirks simply shook his head. "You Catholics," he said.

Busy Morning

A T THE END OF HIS BUSY MORNING, FATHER BROWN decided to carry his newspaper and his cup of tea out to the rectory's porch. He enjoyed sitting there, sometimes reading and sometimes watching the boys and girls play games in the playground across the street. On this occasion his attention to his newspaper was interrupted by the *clack clack* of high heels on the sidewalk. A woman had parked her large blue car in front of the rectory and was now marching purposefully toward the porch.

Even with his weakened eyesight, Father Brown could not help noticing several details about her appearance. He knew nothing of fashion, but her clothing seemed to him of a more expensive style than the women of St. Dominic's wear on a Saturday morning. Her face was heavy with makeup, and her expression was strained, or so it appeared in the harsh midday sun. The priest realized, however, that in the evening, in the softer lighting of a ballroom or dining hall, the same makeup would undoubtedly enhance rather than hide her natural beauty. He leaned on his cane and started to rise.

"Oh, please don't stand, Father," the woman said in a cheery voice. "Let me sit with you instead, and I'll introduce myself. I'm Patricia Evans."

Father Brown found he enjoyed that sort of American informality, especially now that he was in his nineties and jumping to his feet was no longer the effortless action it once had been. He settled back in his chair. "My name is Brown," he said. "I'm the assistant pastor here."

Miss Evans explained that she was hoping to find Father Bell free for a short visit. She was in town on business, but she had promised one of Father Bell's former friends that she would stop by to pass along his best wishes and to give him an important message.

"Father Bell is attending a conference with the bishop and other pastors from this diocese," Father Brown explained. "I'm terribly sorry."

"Well, that's the breaks," Miss Evans said. "I should have phoned first, but if you don't mind, I'll ask you to pass the message along to Father Bell." Then, after glancing at the headline on the front page of the priest's newspaper, she said, "I see you are catching up on the news of that awful murder."

"Yes," the priest replied, "it does have those sensational elements so beloved by newspaper reporters and their editors."

According to the *Sentinel* story, on the previous evening an elderly widower named Otis Radcliffe had been shot to death in his spacious home located in a wooded area in the southern part of the county. The coroner's report stated that the man had been shot in the back four times at close range, and that, after he had collapsed on the floor, he was shot one more time in the back of the head from point-blank range. The weapon, which had been discarded at the scene by the assailant, was a .38-caliber five-shot snub-nosed Smith and Wesson revolver. It was a tiny pistol, weighing less than a pound.

The sheriff's department was investigating, but they were at a loss to explain how the killer had evaded Radcliffe's highly sophisticated security system. Furthermore, since nothing appeared to have been stolen, they did not have any evidence that would point to a motive. Sheriff Dirks was quoted at some length to the effect that the killer might have been a trusted friend with a personal grudge of some kind.

"Yes, it's a sensational crime, Father Brown," Miss Evans was saying, "but it's also quite sad. I met Mr. Radcliffe briefly last night at the Rotary benefit, and my first impression was that he was a very nice and considerate man."

"I'm afraid I never met him," Father Brown said.

"Do you have a guess about what the motive might have been?" Miss Evans asked.

As Sheriff Dirks had spent two hours with Father Brown earlier that morning, the priest knew very well that Radcliffe had a dark past and that he made his fortune during his former life as a crime-syndicate operative. Father Brown had made it his practice never to discuss the conversations or consultations he might have had with the sheriff, however. The one exception was his confessor, Father Bell, who could be trusted not to carry tales.

"I'm afraid we'll have to leave that for the police to decide," Father Brown said.

At this point the rectory housekeeper, the ever hospitable Mrs. James, appeared at the door and asked if Father Brown would like to offer his guest some tea or other refreshment.

"I'll not take more of your time, Father," Miss Evans said, standing up.

"Well then, Mrs. James," the priest said, "please just take these things away, and be sure to type up my notes as usual." Then he took out his pen and jotted something in the margin of the newspaper and laid the items aside.

After a moment's hesitation, Mrs. James removed the tea tray and newspaper from the table and returned to her duties in the rectory.

"And again, please don't bother to stand," Miss Evans said, leaning over the table and extending her hand. "I've enjoyed our chat, and when I return here, I'll be sure to stop in again."

Father Brown watched as her car pulled away from the curb and disappeared down the street.

■   ■   ■

Except for a brief phone conversation, Father Brown did not speak with his friend Sheriff Dirks again until several days had passed. On Wednesday evening, with his investigation now winding down, Dirks was happy to relax in the rectory parlor and accept the glass of Bordeaux Mrs. James offered.

"Let me offer a toast," he said, raising his glass. "Here's to my two honorary assistants, Detectives Brown and James."

"Such foolishness," Mrs. James said as she left the room, but she seemed pleased by the compliment.

"We arrested her as she was checking out of the Royal Hotel," Dirks explained to Father Brown. "We're holding her on suspicion, but with the help of the Feds we're going to prove that this Radcliffe thing was a professional hit. This gal's been operating as a mob assassin for some years, and she did her homework for this job, that's for sure. I think what got us off the track was that she just doesn't look the part."

"I suppose," Father Brown said, "that someone who looks the part would have a more difficult time doing that sort of work than someone whose looks suggest innocence."

"Agreed, Father, but then what put you on to her?"

"It was not her appearance or anything she said," Father Brown replied. "I was just trying to imagine what sort of argument or excuse would cause the late Mr. Radcliffe to suddenly become as careless as he was. Certainly he would not open his door to anyone who looked like a cinema-film assassin."

"You thought he might open his door to a good-looking woman?"

"The thought had crossed my mind as a possibility, especially since you described the revolver as a woman's weapon, something that would fit easily into a woman's small purse."

"I still don't see why you suspected this particular gal—what did she call herself?—this Patricia Evans."

"I didn't suspect her in the least until the moment she left here. It was only then that I realized she had come because she somehow knew that you and I often discussed your cases. In that light, her conversation could be interpreted in a new way. For one thing, she wanted to advance the idea—just in case her private conversation with Mr. Radcliffe at the benefit had been noticed—that nothing had passed between them that was not offhand and innocent. And, secondly, she seemed to be trying to coax me for information about your investigation. When she saw I wasn't going to tell her anything about it, she left quite abruptly. Fortunately I was able to get that note to Mrs. James asking her to copy down the lady's motorcar license number. My eyesight isn't quite up to that sort of task these days."

"And that's all you had?" Dirks asked in surprise. "Father, it seems to me you had a pretty thin basis for suspicion let alone an outright accusation, if you don't mind me saying so."

"The key was not what she said, Sheriff," Father Brown replied, "but what she didn't say. She had told me her one reason for visiting us was to deliver an important message for Father Bell. She left without delivering it.

The Raid

FATHER BROWN TURNED OFF HIS RADIO WITH A SCOWL. The old priest at first had been delighted with the newscast that reported how his friend, Sheriff Dirks, carried out a major drug raid with such great success. A house in the north end of the sleepy Midwest community had been used for some time as a warehouse for large quantities of illegal drugs, and the retail sales value of the stash was, for the time being, beyond calculation. What made Father Brown frown and run his fingers through his stubby white hair was not the success of the operation, but rather its partial failure.

He saw no other way of helping his sheriff friend than to go to the crime scene immediately, and he had no trouble in persuading Father Bell to drive him there. He did not try to find Sheriff Dirks at the newly uncovered drug warehouse, however. He began instead, with knobby cane in hand and Father Bell at his elbow, to ring doorbells in the neighborhood. At last they found what Father Brown had hoped for, a woman who lived across the street from the drug dealer and who could remember back to the time when that house was new. Mrs. Hamm was, if anything, more talkative than need be for Father Brown's purposes, but they found it impossible to escape until she had told the entire story.

This story, according to Mrs. Hamm, began with the first owner, a former navy man originally from Florida. He had been stationed at the Great Lakes Naval Training Center and decided he liked the climate in the Midwest with its changing seasons. A local Bardo County restaurant took him on as an assistant chef, the trade he had learned in the navy. After several years, however, he and his wife decided they missed the warm, snow-free winters and balmy gulf breezes of Tampa. They sold the home and headed back south.

The two who moved in next were very neighborly and sociable, at least in Mrs. Hamm's opinion. The husband, Al, earned his living as a cabinetmaker and was able to build and install fancy new windows and doors; he kept the place in general good repair. He also had a hobby of sleight-of-hand tricks, Mrs. Hamm recalled, with which he delighted the children of the neighborhood.

When Al found a better job in Indianapolis, he sold the house to an older couple from Des Moines who wanted to live near their grandchildren. These folks were quiet neighbors for the most part, but when they entertained houseguests, it was a different story. The new owners' friends from Iowa enjoyed loud parties from sunset in the evening until sunrise in the morning. The two priests suspected that Mrs. Hamm enjoyed exaggerating things for the sake of a good story.

These neighbors moved out when the husband's health failed and he required the all-embracing care provided by nursing homes. After his wife found an apartment near her husband's care facility, she sold the house to the current owner, the man who had been so recently exposed as a drug dealer. "He is not neighborly at all," Mrs. Hamm explained at some length and in great detail. At last Father Brown was able to bid the lady goodbye with his profuse thanks, and the two priests headed across the street to find Father Brown's friend.

"Just the man I want to see," Dirks said, inviting them into the house. "I'm in a jam."

"We heard about it on the radio," Father Brown said.

"The big fish that got away," Father Bell added.

"Yeah, he got away," the sheriff said ruefully, "but this time it really is impossible." Then Dirks described the raid, which he had conducted himself with the help of five deputies.

"We had the place surrounded," he said, "but before we could make our move, the Channel Two helicopter from the city comes and hovers over the house. That nosey old bag across the street must have phoned them with the tip. She probably thought she'd get her mug on the six o'clock news. Anyway, this guy we're after starts out the front door to see what's making all that racket above his house, and naturally the first thing he sees is me. So he pops back into the house, and I was right behind him."

"And you couldn't find him in the house?" Father Bell asked.

"Here's the thing, Father Bell," Dirks said. "Not only did we have the place surrounded, but the helicopter caught the whole thing on videotape. I've seen it. It shows all four sides of the house. Nobody left the place. Look around here—there are no trees or cover of any kind."

While Father Bell continued the conversation, Father Brown's thoughts seemed to be elsewhere. At length he said, "Sheriff, please get a couple of your men in here right away. And please tell them to be ready with their guns."

■   ■   ■

That night, the three men enjoyed a celebratory drink in the parlor of St. Dominic's rectory. Father Brown sipped a glass of dry sherry while Sheriff Dirks and Father Bell had decided on beer, which Mrs. James was pleased to serve in frosted steins.

"Now will you tell me how you figured this one out?" Dirks asked. "You made me a hero today, Father Brown. And I was doing my best to make myself a laughing stock."

"Well, when I heard the radio report," Father Brown said, "the facts made no sense. I began by wondering what *would* make sense. I wondered how it might be possible that the fugitive could still be in the house. That's when I decided I needed to know more about the house. Rather than study the place itself, which I knew you had done in minute detail, I thought I might learn something from the neighbors about it and the people who had lived in it.

"It was just luck that we found that friendly and talkative woman across the way, and she knew every detail of the house's history. She told us of a former resident, a cabinetmaker, who had a hobby of conjuring. That set me to wondering if he ever gave magic shows in his living room. I wondered if his act might have gone beyond card tricks. I ended by thinking part of his act might have been to make his wife vanish or appear from nowhere."

"I see it now," Dirks said. "He was a cabinetmaker. He made that secret door through the living room wall into the bedroom, with enough room in the wall itself to hide a supply of illegal drugs, and it was plenty big enough for a person to hide in."

"As I admitted before," Father Brown said, "we were lucky. The drug dealer's residence just might be the only house in America with a genuine priest's hole."

"Priest's hole!" said Dirks. "Listen, I've seen enough spooky movies to know that every English mansion worthy of the name has all kinds of secret panels and hidden rooms, but I never heard them called 'priest's holes' before."

"It all depends upon who is the enemy of the people," Father Brown answered. "In our day you chase after drug dealers. In Shakespeare's day you would have been busy hunting down Roman Catholic priests."

"If that's true," Dirks protested, "why didn't I hear about it in history class?"

Father Bell smiled and returned the question. "Why, indeed?" he asked

The Birthday Gift

BILL KELLER PEERED OVER THE SIDE OF THE ROOF. SIX floors below him nothing could be seen in the darkness but street lamps and the headlights of passing cars. After he had tied his rope ladder to a secure stanchion, he quietly dropped the loose end over the edge and lowered himself into position for the climb down. Some in law enforcement might have referred to him as a "second-story man," but he preferred the more romantic title of "cat burglar."

Bill had been at it for fifteen years, and he could honestly boast that he had never been caught and, indeed, had never even had a close call. He did not attribute this to luck, but rather to good information, careful planning, and an unwillingness to take unnecessary risks. He plied his trade in small Midwest towns where the police were unsophisticated, and where most householders did not bother to install the high-tech security systems so popular in the big cities. After three burglaries, and long before the police would notice any pattern in the seemingly random break-ins, he would be off to another town.

Bill stopped his descent at the level of the fourth floor and looked through a window into a bathroom. The light was on and the door was closed. All to the good, he thought. He knew for certain no one was in the apartment.

He hadn't had to do much planning for this job, because he had been lucky—lucky beyond the bounds of anything he had ever experienced. Most of the information had been a gift, dropped into his lap yesterday purely by accident. He was in the café of his hotel enjoying a solitary lunch, when the conversation behind him caught his ear. What was the woman saying?

"Oh, you wouldn't believe what he keeps around just as knickknacks," she said. "The rest of us have a plastic box to keep our paperclips in. He's got a beautifully carved and jeweled ivory case for his paperclips, and it's worth a month's salary for us ordinary mortals." Bill dropped his napkin and as he retrieved it from the floor he stole a backward glance. He saw two middle-aged women having a good gossip while they lunched.

"He loves little gold things, too," the woman gushed, "and things ornamented with precious stones. He likes anything that's delicate, old, and expensive. And why not?" she asked herself. "He's worked hard for his success and his money."

That was yesterday. Now, Bill was busy cutting out the bottom pane of the bathroom window while hanging four stories above the pavement. As he worked, he held the glass securely with a special set of suction cups. Then he dropped the glass rectangle into the cloth bag that he had tied to the rope ladder. Letting the glass fall to the street might get someone's attention. Even though he was dressed in black from head to toe, he did not want anyone looking too closely at the upper stories of this building.

Yesterday, the ladies had continued their discussion of the rich man with the expensive trinkets. Bill pushed his chair back from the table and turned his head slightly, desperate to catch every word. The talkative woman, he learned, was the man's private secretary, and by bragging about his wealth and possessions, she was attempting to bask a bit in his reflected glory. When the other woman asked, "Just where is this fabulous condo of his?" Bill strained to hear the answer, not daring to breathe.

But now he was angling himself into the man's bathroom, feet first while facing away from the building. He lowered himself noiselessly to the floor and listened. Not a sound. He pulled on a pair of tight-fitting plastic surgeon's gloves. The cops would find no telltale fingerprints after this job, he thought with satisfaction. Then he looked around and saw the gold-plated bathroom fixtures. That babblermouth secretary's tip-offs were beginning to look like the jackpot.

She had yammered on and on about her wonderful boss and how he would be celebrating his fiftieth birthday the very next day. "Mr. Connor lives by himself now that he's divorced," she said. "He's invited all of his friends to a dinner party at the country club. It's tomorrow at eight." Bill had to ask himself if he had ever in his life gathered so much useful information so quickly and so easily. A bit of research on the building, and he'd have the job planned. The woman would never know that for her boss's birthday she had handed the biggest gift to Bill.

He turned off the light and slowly opened the bathroom door. The apartment was as dark and as quiet as a mausoleum. He crept soundlessly away from the bedrooms, around a corner, and down the hallway. When he was a few steps from the living room, he unhooked a sizeable leather bag from his belt and reached for his pencil-thin flashlight.

Bill worked quickly, beginning as always with any valuables that could be swooped into his bag from tabletops and side-boards. Then he stopped and listened. Something was wrong.

He had the intense feeling that he was not alone. He thought he heard a faint rustling noise. He stood still, afraid to breathe. Then to his horror the lights in the large room blazed and he saw a tall man standing by the light switch, his arm bent at the elbow and his hand pointing an ugly-looking pistol toward the ceiling.

"Sheriff's Police," the man said in a flat voice. "Don't do anything silly. I'm Sheriff Dirks." Bill glanced over his shoulder and saw a second man, short and burly shouldered, leaning lazily against the wall behind him. "That's Deputy O'Malley."

"Pleased to meet you," O'Malley said. "Hands behind your back. I'll take that bag." He clamped a pair of handcuffs around Bill's wrists. "You are under arrest," he said without emphasis.

"I guess my luck just ran out," Bill said.

"Not luck," the deputy said. "Believe me, Buddy, you goofed, big time."

"It was a set up?" Bill asked.

"Nothing like that," said the sheriff. "You had lunch at the Royal Hotel yesterday. You probably didn't notice the two men at a nearby table, but they noticed you. At least the older one noticed you—my good friend, a Catholic priest named Brown. He saw how you were practically sitting in that woman's lap trying to overhear her conversation, and he decided he had better find out what was so interesting.

"When he heard what the lady was saying, he knew your angle right away, and he dialed me up from the hotel lobby. You came straight here to check this place out, and O'Malley and I were here ahead of you. We watched every move you made while you studied this building. And I'll tell you this, I've never met anybody in police work who understands how a criminal's mind works the way this clergyman does. I'm just glad he didn't choose a life of crime. He'd have been unstoppable."

The shorter man laughed and said, "We phoned Connor, the guy who owns this condo. I told him we had a birthday gift for him. He got a buzz out of that, believe me."

"Birthday gift," Bill repeated.

"You have the right to remain silent," Dirks intoned. "You have the right t—"

The Agency's Star

SHERIFF DIRKS FOUND HIMSELF WONDERING WHETHER a solution was even possible in this maddening puzzle of a murder case. The basic facts were simple enough. An advertising executive named Alan Barr had been found slumped over his desk with a slim metal letter opener lodged between his shoulder blades. Barr had been stabbed from behind—five times—and one of these thrusts had found his heart. The problem was, the victim had locked himself in his office, and no one had been with him when he was attacked. It was impossible, but...

Father Brown invited Dirks to sit at a small table in the rectory's comfortable kitchen. "Stabbed five times from behind," the priest said. "That must have been done in a burst of uncontrollable fury." The sheriff nodded in agreement. "But tell me something about the victim, Sheriff."

"He was the agency's star salesman," Dirks said, "and a winner according to all reports. The customers loved him. They considered him a true friend. I'm told they were always entertaining him in their homes, inviting him to play golf, and that sort of thing. His colleagues in the agency felt the same way, but the people who thought of him as a boss talked about him as though he were more of a taskmaster than a friend.

Still, he got the job done—I said he was a winner—and he had everyone's respect."

"What happened?" Father Brown asked.

"It was the morning before a big sales presentation," Dirks replied. "It was the usual thing for Barr to lock himself in his office and have his secretary cancel his appointments and hold his phone calls. Then he would write his presentation and practice it until he had it perfect. They say he was the grandmaster of the sales pitch."

The priest considered this, and then asked, "How do you know he didn't let someone into his office when no one was looking? When the intruder left, wouldn't the door automatically lock when he shut it? It seems obvious that something like that must have happened."

"Well, Barr's secretary, Wanda Meier, is probably as reliable a witness as you could ask for, although she was extremely upset. Anyhow, we don't have to depend on her testimony even though everybody says she's the most efficient secretary in the world. We have other witnesses saying exactly what she said."

"I know Wanda well," said Father Brown. "She's a widow. She's a loyal member of our parish."

"Anyhow," Dirks continued, "Wanda tells me Barr never let anyone interrupt him when he was rehearsing. He had buzzed her on the intercom at eleven that morning and asked her to cancel his lunch date. She says she stayed at her desk between the time of his intercom call and the time they found him dead. She says nobody went in or out of his office. See, Father, no one could have gotten into that office without pounding on the door and shouting or at least speaking loudly. If that had happened, people nearby would have noticed, but nobody noticed anything like that. In fact, when they finally did go into Barr's office, the commotion attracted a whole crowd of witnesses."

"Or cloud of witnesses," Father Brown said with a smile, and then more seriously he added, "What made them decide to enter his office?"

"The agency's president showed up and said it was an emergency," Dirks said. "They tried to get Barr on the intercom, and when he wouldn't answer they had the custodian unlock the door. They found him dead."

"How was this office laid out?"

"You want to figure out where the killer was hiding," Dirks said with a grin that turned quickly to a frown. He described the room's Spartan style, which included a simple table that served as Barr's desk, a few chairs of Danish design, a coffee caddie, and abstract pictures on the walls—a room without filing cabinets or clutter or even a sofa to crouch behind or a closet to hide in.

"You couldn't conceal anything bigger than a breadbox in there," Dirks said. "The windows weren't made to be opened. If you think the killer was hiding behind the drapes, well, there are no drapes, just blinds. And the blinds were raised."

Dirks went on to explain that the agency is a small-sized business firm, and there aren't a whole lot of employees working there. In any case, they operate in teams and have a lot of meetings, and everybody who was working in the agency at the crucial time was with three or four other people. Dirks told Father Brown that there were a few visitors—a couple of salesmen and some repairmen—but that their movements were fully accounted for.

"There are two people who had a special dislike for Barr," Dirks said, "the custodian and the mail boy. They do move around on their own, but the custodian was installing some file cabinets in plain sight of witnesses; and the mail boy, who by the way is sixty-three years young, had sneaked down to the first floor cocktail lounge to stoke up on liquid nourishment. The bartender backs up his story."

"If I sum up what you've told me," Father Brown said, "the victim, a man beloved of his colleagues, was found stabbed to death in a room that had but one door, which was securely locked and closely watched. Several witnesses swear that there were no visitors inside his office when the custodian unlocked the door. There is no other way out, and there is nowhere in the room to hide. Is that accurate?"

"That's right," Dirks said. "And now I suppose you're going to congratulate me on finding all the facts that point to the killer, and you'll be charitable enough to excuse me for not seeing the obvious. Well, I'm used to that, Father Brown."

"No," the priest answered solemnly. "From the way you've described the facts, I am not going to be able to give you your answer."

"Well, there's one consolation in that, at least," said Dirks. "There are times when even you are stumped."

"I am truly sorry," said Father Brown.

■   ■   ■

Father Brown's careful response to the sheriff did not precisely mean that he was stumped. After careful thought and prayer, he decided to ask Wanda Meier to visit him at the rectory so that he might discuss what had happened directly with her.

He was never one for needless preliminaries. "Mrs. Meier," he began, "you and I know that there was one person who would be admitted into that office without fanfare." The secretary shook her head and seemed not to understand.

"That person," Father Brown continued, "had more reason than anyone to hate 'the agency's star', the grandmaster of salesmanship, a man everyone looked up to with respect and admiration. However, the person I have in mind knew this man best for what he was—an insufferable tyrant and bully. Never getting a kind word between insults will build up resentment, and sometimes there is an explosion.

"Your crime was not premeditated, Mrs. Meier," Father Brown said. "The decision is yours, but if you choose to reveal these things to the sheriff, I think Father Bell and I can persuade him to be easy on you—I mean easy with the formal and legal charges."

The two talked on, but what they said next is hidden from us by the seal of the sacrament of reconciliation, which Father Brown still referred to as "the sacrament of penance" and Wanda Meier thought of simply as "confession."

On the following morning, Sheriff Dirks looked on in surprise as two Catholic priests and a private secretary walked slowly through his open door and stood uncomfortably and somberly before him.

Security Camera

FAMOUS EVANGELIST MURDERED AT CLASS REUNION," the headlines blared. Such a high profile case could not be left in the hands of a "hick" law enforcement department—as even Sheriff Dirks had to admit. He was happy the FBI had stepped in.

"The Feds will solve it eventually," he said, "but for the time being even those guys are baffled."

"Tell me about it," said Father Brown.

The sheriff was sitting in a comfortable chair in the rectory parlor, discussing his latest case with his friend, the very old but very wise associate pastor of St. Dominic's parish. "It all revolves around a security camera," Dirks said, gesturing with his large hands and long arms. "It seems to prove that Reverend Roland was alone when he was bludgeoned to death. How's that for a mystery? Anyhow, the preacher's death was not entirely unexpected. He had been getting death threats from some fanatics who said the charity money he collects mostly goes into his own pockets. That is true enough—he skimmed millions."

"You're sure of this?" Father Brown asked.

"Yeah, I'm sure. It's amazing what the FBI can find out in a short time. But they say it was all legally proper."

"Of course. And did the FBI also say it was morally proper?"

"No, that's your bailiwick, Father Brown," Dirks said, with a broad grin. He then explained that Roland's wife had put his security plan together for him because she had worked for a security firm before they were married. In fact, as Dirks had learned from FBI reports, her salary had paid for Roland's divinity school education and she now worked from their home, scheduling the preacher's evangelical performances, handling his travel plans, and keeping the books.

"Anyhow, Roland was my size, about six-foot-four, and Mrs. Roland hired three bodyguards to travel with him, all about that height. She thought they'd look puny if they were shorter than her husband, and she made them wear trench coats and black fedoras. She said she wanted them to look menacing! And sometimes she hired extra help locally. She put Shorty Means on the job here."

"Why, he's not much taller than me," said Father Brown.

Dirks chose to ignore this comment. "When Roland is on the road, he takes along a state-of-the-art security camera," he continued. "The camera sits in his hotel room. They aim it at the inside of the door for a record of anyone coming in or going out. But, you know, I could be wrong, but I think the wife included it in the security plan just to discourage Roland from having ladies in his room."

"He was an unfaithful husband?"

Dirks then explained that, indeed, the evangelist did have that unfortunate reputation, and at the class reunion witnesses said that he had been flirting with a former classmate of his named Lana Bern—a divorcée and, by all accounts, a beautiful woman.

"I was frankly surprised," the sheriff said, "when Lana told me she is actually closer to Mrs. Roland than she was to the preacher."

"Is Reverend Roland's wife also a real beauty?" Father Brown asked.

"No way," Dirks said. "She's just a plain Jane who wears thrift-shop dresses. You know, Lana often stayed with her when the preacher was on the road. The FBI says that part of her story checks out.

"But back to the case, Father. Here's what the witnesses say, and it's supported by what we see on the videotape record from the security camera. When the reunion party broke up, most of the people went into the bar for a nightcap, but Roland bowed out." Father Brown's raised eyebrows showed his surprise at this information. "Well, Father, he was a teetotaler. But anyhow, the tape shows him and a bodyguard entering his room at ten minutes after ten. The two of them searched his room for any thugs lurking in the shower stall and so on—part of the routine the preacher's wife dreamed up. Then the tape shows the guard leaving the room. He says he stood sentry until Shorty relieved him at two in the morning. He says he heard no sounds coming from the room."

As the medical examiner had put the time of death at between eleven and midnight, Roland, the sheriff argued, must have been dead in his room by the time Shorty arrived for duty. Shorty knew nothing about the death, and so he faithfully guarded the door to Roland's room until one of the bodyguards arrived at five in the morning accompanied by the desk clerk. The bodyguard said that he had tried telephoning Roland to wake him up and had not gotten an answer. After the clerk used his passkey, the sheriff explained, the three men each said they saw Roland on the bed with his legs sticking out from under the covers. The man was still in his trousers from the night before. Then Roland's bodyguard told the other two to wait in the doorway while he searched the room. He announced to them that Roland was stone dead. As the sheriff learned later, he had been dead for hours.

"The tall guy searched the room," the sheriff continued, "but that's a laugh—you can't hide a kitten in there—and then he guarded the door while Shorty and the clerk looked around. That was smart because it makes three witnesses telling the same story. But the tall guy wouldn't let them touch anything, and that was smart, too."

"And that's when they telephoned you?" the priest asked.

"No, they didn't want anything in the room disturbed including the phone. Shorty and the clerk went down to the front desk and called us from there. When I arrived, the three tall guys were outside the room holding back the gapers. We checked the room and saw that the windows can't be opened, and there's no place for anybody to hide. The back of Pastor Roland's head was smashed in. No sign of a weapon.

"The videotape shows nothing but a shut door from ten-fifteen at night to five in the morning. The FBI took the tape and camera for analysis because they think it was tampered with somehow. But I doubt it."

"Wasn't the camera's view sometimes blocked when Shorty and the other men walked past it to search the room?" Father Brown asked.

Dirks was losing patience with Father Brown's seeming inability to follow the plain facts of the case. "Yeah, but Father," he replied, "nobody ever stood in the way for more than a second or two, and that was hours after the murder. That door stayed shut from before the murder 'till early morning. The videotape proves it. I know it seems impossible, but those are the facts." But then the gleam in the priest's eye caught the sheriff's attention. He had seen that gleam many times before. "What is it, Father?" he asked.

"As you explain those facts," the priest replied, "the case is extremely complicated. Let us see whether or not I have gotten these facts straight in my mind."

Father Brown then reviewed the case as Dirks had described it. Roland, in the company of one of his guards, had returned to his room shortly after ten o'clock. After searching the room, the guard left, presumably to stand sentry outside the door. He was relieved of that responsibility by Shorty Means at two the following morning. The desk clerk, Shorty, and one of the guards entered the room at six. They all agree that Roland was alone in a room that was securely locked from the inside and that he was dead.

"Is that the story as you've explained it to me?" Father Brown asked.

"Yes," Dirks replied, "and it's backed up by witnesses and the security camera."

"I think not."

"You don't believe the security camera?"

"It's not the security camera," Father Brown said. "I'm not thinking of that. I'm thinking of a millionaire who keeps his wife in cheap dresses. A clergyman who breaks his marriage vows and steals money from his flock. A traveling man who will not permit his wife to accompany him, even to his class reunion."

"But, Father Brown, what does all of that mean?" Dirks asked. "What do you think it adds up to?"

"I was merely wondering what this woman might discuss with her close friend during her wealthy husband's long absences."

"You mean murder?" said Dirks. He leaned forward in his chair, afraid he might miss even one word.

"Let us say they began by sending the hate mail—an excuse for hiring three ruffians who will do anything for money. It would be easy, I suppose, for an attractive woman like this Lana

Bern to persuade Roland to meet her after the party—in her room. Easy, while she distracted him, for one of the bodyguards to strike him dead."

"But the security camera," Dirks protested.

"Wouldn't Roland, with his back to the camera, leaving the room shortly after ten o'clock, with trench coat and fedora, look just like one of his own bodyguards?"

Dirks stared at the priest for several minutes, his mind racing. At length he said, "I think I can finish this story, Father. It was Roland, not the bodyguard, who the camera showed leaving the room at ten-ten. When Shorty and the desk clerk and the tall guy opened Roland's door at five, it was another one of the bodyguards, not Roland, playing possum in Roland's bed. Then, when Shorty and the clerk went downstairs to phone us, two of the bodyguards brought the preacher's body from Lana's room using her bedclothes as a kind of stretcher. The bedclothes would carry the trace evidence forensics looks for. The third bodyguard blocked the camera for a few seconds every time they had to go through that door. It was an ingenious plan."

"Yes," said Father Brown, "but I cannot admire them for that. I can understand anger, resentment, and bitter hurt, but these ladies seem to have done this for the money. Their scheme was brilliantly conceived and artfully carried through. It was a work born of a high level of genius, but I fear the motive for doing it issued from a lower region of inspiration."

He shook his head and shuddered as if he were trying to rid his mind of something unclean. "Far lower," he said.

Father Brown's Tale

THOUGH NOW IN HIS NINETIES, FATHER BROWN WAS still in good health and full of vigor, and he always enjoyed his quiet chats with his friend Sheriff Dirks. At his age, Father Brown much preferred talking about criminals to his older hobby of chasing them.

The sheriff was comfortably seated in an overstuffed chair, and he looked with pleasure at the large tumbler full of cold diet cola that Mrs. James, the housekeeper, kept on hand especially for him—for neither of the two resident priests cared for that sort of beverage.

"This is about two brothers, Gabriel and Ben Garland," he began. "They own a downtown drugstore together, or at least they did before Gabriel was found dead in his office. A druggist, you know, has no trouble getting hold of lethal doses of fast-acting poison, and the hypodermic needle that did the job on Gabriel was found clasped in his hand. But my problem is that some evidence points to suicide and other evidence points to murder. And it's either suicide or murder," Dirks said. "It can't be both."

"Oh?" said Father Brown. He stared at the carpet for several minutes before he spoke again. "May I tell you a story, Sheriff?"

he asked. "It's a kind of cautionary tale about a curious problem in logic. I can't promise it will help you, but it might."

"I'm all ears," said Dirks.

"My tale is set some time ago in the Canadian Rocky Mountains," said Father Brown. "It happened one night in the midst of a winter ice storm. A man was killed when his motorcar plunged over the edge of a mountain road. The police investigation found that the motorcar had skidded out of control while rounding a curve, and the tire marks showed how the driver had tried valiantly to right the vehicle and how he had failed. It was clearly an accident, although—as with many accidents—this one sprang from reckless behavior and might have been avoided.

"It later came to light that the police had been on the verge of arresting this man for embezzlement. It was said that he would have been convicted easily on the evidence. Then the police found a suicide note in which the man stated that life was no longer worth living. His friends testified that he had been terribly despondent. So you see, Sheriff, his death was clearly a suicide, although he chose to end his life by driving carelessly over a treacherous road."

"Yes, I see," Dirks said.

"Ah, but there is more," said Father Brown. "After several years it was revealed—never mind how—that this man had not really been guilty of embezzlement. In truth, the evidence against him had been manufactured by his ruthless business partner. The threats of the partner had driven him to the brink of suicide.

"But although the man was desperate to die, he was not capable of deliberately ending his own life, and so the evil partner suggested he take that fatal automobile ride through the storm over the dangerous mountain roads."

"Why it was a form of murder then," Dirks said with surprise.

"Yes, *murder*," the priest answered, "though the murderer's method was to drive the victim to commit *suicide* though the agency of a motoring *accident*."

"Wow," said Dirks. "So, it doesn't have to be one thing or another after all."

"Have you time for another glass of fizzy soda?" the priest asked.

"Thanks, no," Dirks said. "Obviously, I've got work to do, and I better get hopping."

■   ■   ■

A month passed before Sheriff Dirks stopped at the rectory for another visit with Father Brown. He was again seated in the comfortable study, and Mrs. James was not tardy in serving them refreshments.

"To your good health," said Father Brown.

"And yours," said Dirks. "Look, I wanted to tell you how the business about the death of that druggist was resolved." Father Brown merely nodded.

"We had just arrested Gabriel's brother Ben on suspicion of murder," said Dirks. "But then Gabriel's widow and her lawyer came to see us. She told us that she and her husband had been conspiring to poison his brother. You see, things were set up so that if one brother died, the other brother would own the whole drugstore business. The store profits had been in a slow decline for some years, and the motive that pushed Gabriel and his wife to plan the murder of his brother was plain and simple greed.

"Well, Father, the best laid plans, and so on. Gabriel carelessly stabbed himself with the hypodermic he was readying for his brother, and the fast-acting poison did the rest. When I said it was either murder or suicide, I was wrong. The truth is, the possibility of an accident had never crossed my mind." The priest said nothing.

"Still, Father," Dirks continued, "that tale you told me about the accident in the Canadian mountains shows that *you* had it all figured out; and for once, I know how you knew it without you giving me the explanation. Gabriel's widow belongs to St. Dominic's parish, and she told us that she confessed to you, Father Brown; she says you warned her that if an innocent man was ever falsely accused of Gabriel's murder, she would be morally obliged to come to us with the truth. That's what she did, and so the case is wrapped up and put to bed.

"You tried to tip me off with that tale of yours, Father. But you couldn't be direct because you priests can't reveal the secrets of confession." The sheriff's grin showed he was proud of this deduction.

"Sheriff," said Father Brown, "the day you told me about this drugstore poisoning case was the first time I had ever heard a word about it."

"But—but then," the Sheriff sputtered, "if you didn't have the facts, how did you know enough to concoct that tale of yours?"

"The tale had nothing to do with facts," answered Father Brown. "It had to do with logic."

"At least," said the sheriff, "you'll have to admit Mrs. Garland came to you later and confessed how she and her husband had planned the murder of his brother. I guess that must have been sometime after we had our discussion about the case. She did confess it to you, didn't she?"

The priest's expression was unreadable. "Did I ever tell you about my first murder?" he asked. "It was just a small private affair in the city of Paris. The killer cut off the head of one of his dinner guests with a soldier's saber. Have another glass of fizzy soda, Sheriff, and I'll tell you all about it. It makes quite a tale."

Nickname

EVER SINCE SHERIFF DIRKS HAD ASSUMED THE DUTIES of sheriff, his office had been plagued by more than its fair share of puzzling crimes. Dirks knew he could not have solved any of these cases without the help of his friend Father Brown. Now in his nineties, the priest was far too old to be chasing after criminals himself, but he enjoyed the challenge of unraveling the sheriff's riddles from the comfort of his armchair.

The sheriff's latest murder had just the note of impossibility that always confounded him but just as often proved transparently simple to Father Brown. A woman had called the emergency number from the Royal Hotel. She was highly distraught, but she managed to convey to the operator that there had been an accidental shooting in room 435 and that an ambulance was urgently needed.

The sheriff's police found room 435 locked, bolted, and chained from the inside. After forcing the door, they discovered the lifeless body of a woman collapsed on the bed and still clutching a blood-soaked pillow to her breast. According to the medical examiner, she had been shot three times in the chest and had died no more than ten minutes before the police arrived. The weapon, a .38-caliber pistol, lay on the carpet. A careful search showed that no one else was in the room.

The windows were also securely locked from the inside. An assailant, if there had been one, could not have left the room without unlocking either the door or one of the windows. The fingerprints on the gun, the phone, and on all the locks were the victim's, as were the prints on the doorknobs inside and out. The inescapable conclusion was that the woman had been alone when she was shot.

Suicide was ruled out because no gunshot residue was found on the victim's hands or clothing, and forensics determined that the shots had been fired from a distance of at least six feet. A firearm when thrown or dropped will often discharge when it strikes the floor. What no one could explain was how this gun, which was not an automatic, could have fired three accurate shots by that sort of accident.

After the sheriff and his deputies had ruled out homicide, suicide, and accidental death, they were left with the embarrassment of a shooting fatality they could not explain even in theory.

"Who was this woman?" Father Brown asked. Sheriff Dirks had accepted the priest's offer of coffee, and now the two men were comfortably seated at a table in the rectory kitchen.

"Her name was Mary Wren," Dirks said. "Her husband Tom was staying at the Deluxe Motel here in town." Seeing Father Brown's expression, he added, "It was a badly failing marriage, Father. From what I can piece together, Mary had every reason in the world to shoot the man, but he had no cause whatsoever to attack her.

"Tom was an abusive husband—tyrannical, vicious, a drunkard, and chronically unfaithful. He can't hold a job, and he's been sponging off Mary for years. The pattern is this: Tom goes to a bar and looks for a female with interests in line with his own. The two run off together, and eventually Mary follows after them. That's what happened this time. The pistol belongs to Tom, by the way, but we think Mary brought it with her because she was planning to use it on the other woman or possibly on her husband. Anyway, we know she had the weapon in her room."

"What is the husband's version of these events?" Father Brown asked.

"He says he was with his girlfriend the whole time. She backs him up. The jerk went out of his way to tell me he's glad to be rid of his worthless wife. He says he's going to marry the girlfriend. When I questioned them, Father, they weren't what I would call completely sober."

"Well, Sheriff," said Father Brown, "I am as baffled as you are. I am truly sorry."

Dirks frowned and looked down at his shoes. "If anything pops into your head, let me know," he said. "I've already interviewed Zelda's friends, and of course their version makes her out to be a saint, but—"

"Wait," Father Brown interrupted. "I thought you said her name was *Mary*."

"For some odd reason her friends nicknamed her Zelda."

"Well, that puts a new spin on things," said Father Brown. "Did her friends by any chance also describe her as cheerful?"

"How on earth..."

"Just so," said the priest. "Now, Sheriff, I believe I can unravel your puzzle for you."

"Because of a nickname?"

"Yes," said Father Brown, "because of a nickname, and now I know what happened in that hotel room as surely as if I had been there. Mary's foolish husband came to the hotel to murder his wife so that he would be free of her. He shot her and left her for dead. It was not only an unspeakably wicked deed, but it was also unbelievably stupid. Under ordinary circumstances,

Sheriff, you would have had him in your jail within an hour of the shooting.

"Mary realized all of this of course. She deliberately put her own fingerprints on his gun to protect him. Then she used the pillow to stanch her wounds while she painfully walked to the door, left her fingerprints on the doorknobs, and locked the door securely. Only then did she phone for help, but too late.

"You see, Sheriff, Mary followed her husband around not to thwart him, but to help him out of trouble. I'm quite sure she often had set bail for him, paid his tavern bills, made apologies, and brought him back home. For this she earned his everlasting resentment."

"But how do you know all of this?"

"Zelda is the shortened form for Griselda," answered Father Brown. "It is the name of a woman in those old medieval tales of a cruel husband whose patient wife bore all of his ill-treatment without complaint. Mary's friends were familiar with the story. They nicknamed her 'Griselda' because they thought she was like the woman in the legend."

"That's a pretty thin line of reasoning based on a very weak clue," said Dirks.

"It's a moral clue, Sheriff, and a strong one," Father Brown replied. "And it is the only line of reasoning that explains the facts. I only regret that these tales and romances of the age of chivalry are no longer taught to our youngsters."

"I suppose it's my duty to follow up on it," Dirks conceded. When the priest did not answer, he added, "I suppose it's your duty to pray for the soul of the deceased."

"Just think of the love this woman had for that worthless wretch of a husband. She gave her life for him. And now that you have reminded me of my duty, Sheriff Dirks, I rather think I might pray to Zelda, or rather Zelda and I might pray together for her husband's conversion."

Dirks found this last idea rather bizarre. After he had wrested confessions from Tom Wren and his girl friend, he returned to the rectory to ask his friend to explain this praying-with-the-dead business.

In the ensuing weeks and months, Dirks often found himself visiting the rectory to discuss subjects other than knotty puzzles of criminology. His tentative new theory was that the old priest might have answers to more mysteries than those under the jurisdiction of the sheriff's department.

The Appointment

J AY SIMONS HAD BEEN DELIGHTED WITH MR. DIAZ. HE didn't mind the man's rather stringent conditions and demands. The hope of selling him a condominium was more than enough to compensate for a few unusual requests. Jay would call upon Mr. Diaz precisely at two in the afternoon, Wednesday. He would not be late, and he would not attempt to change the appointment time. Jay thought these limitations were fair enough considering the size of the deal that was in the offing.

Jay remembered his first impression of Diaz. The man had entered his small real estate and insurance office on Main Street and offered his card. He was average in height and build, dark of complexion, and well dressed in a light-blue business suit that suggested the hand of a tailor. He spoke perfect if somewhat studied English. Most strikingly, the lower half of Diaz's face was hidden behind a thick black beard and mustache. He was, he said, an importer of Mexican jewelry, and he had decided to relocate his business to Jay's hometown, a small and friendly community in the Middle West. Jay was looking forward to a very profitable afternoon.

Jay arrived at the Royal Hotel just before two o'clock, and he knocked on the door of Diaz's suite at precisely that hour. A smiling Diaz opened the door, but he seemed somewhat flustered. He explained with embarrassment that he was behind in his schedule, and that he was discussing business with an associate in the bedroom. He asked Jay to forgive him and to wait another ten minutes. Then, he promised, he and Jay could wrap up their deal.

Jay assured Diaz that this would be no problem whatsoever. He settled on the couch and turned on the TV, which was tuned to a game show. It was about twenty minutes later when a somewhat younger man emerged from the bedroom. "Mr. Diaz makes the apologies for keeping you waiting," the man said. For Jay, his heavy Spanish accent and dark skin marked him as a Mexican—or perhaps a Latino of some other national origin.

"Mr. Diaz asks you to give him the ten minutes more," the man continued. "This he needs to complete the writing and the telephone." Jay assured him that he would wait. He watched as the man left the suite, and then turned his attention back to Bob Barker and "The Price is Right."

By the time "ten minutes more" had stretched to half an hour, Jay began to feel uneasy. He pressed his ear against the door that divided the suite's sitting room from the bath and bedroom section. There was not a sound to be heard. "Mr. Diaz!" he called. He rapped on the door and called again. Then he opened the door.

Juan Diaz lay in a heap on the floor, his handsome new suit hopelessly rumpled. A cord was wound tightly around his neck; and above the black of his beard, his swollen face had turned a ghastly blue.

For a moment Jay was lost in a wave of vertigo, but he fought against it and calmed himself. He knelt down and felt for the man's pulse. Then he dialed 9-1-1 from the sitting room, and there he stayed until the sheriff arrived with two deputies.

Five days later, both Jay and Sheriff Dirks called on Father Brown, an elderly priest whose blinking gray eyes behind owlish spectacles seemed to suggest innocence rather than mature judgment, but whose insightful advice had often earned him the sheriff's praise and immense gratitude. They sat at a small table in the parlor of the rectory of St. Dominic's, and after Jay finished telling his story, Father Brown turned his attention to Sheriff Dirks.

"I can't bring myself to pin this on Jay," Dirks said. "I've known him for twenty-five years. He didn't do it. And we now know that Diaz was a big-time drug runner. The FBI and the ATF were closing in on him, but they lost track of him in Chicago two weeks ago."

Father Brown considered this. "Did anything in the least bit peculiar turn up in your investigations?" he asked. Dirks looked dubious. "Even a small detail?" the priest insisted.

"Well, it's funny that Jay didn't hear any sounds of a struggle," Dirks said, "but strangulation isn't necessarily a noisy sort of way to kill someone. Oh, and not that it's important, but we have two versions of the time Diaz went up to his room. The desk clerk swears he saw him go up at exactly one o'clock, but the bellman insists it was exactly one-thirty. Anyone can see what's going on in that small lobby, but these guys saw two different things."

"Was there anything else?" Father Brown asked.

Dirks shrugged. "Well," he said, "we'll never find a man based on a description of a Hispanic male of medium height and build with black hair and beard and no distinguishing characteristics other than a Spanish accent. Can you guess how many men fit that description in this jurisdiction alone? And we have no reason to suppose the man has stayed in Bardo County. He could be anywhere."

"I may be able to give you a more helpful description," said Father Brown. "This murder of yours was five days ago?"

"Yeah," Dirks said, "but—"

"The name of the man you're looking for," Father Brown said, "is Juan Diaz. No, Sheriff, before you protest, let me explain. Diaz almost certainly has gone back to Chicago; and though he left here clean-shaven, he's now sporting a five-day's growth of black whiskers. He's carrying the identification papers of the man he killed in that hotel bedroom."

The Sheriff and Jay exchanged glances of astonishment, but the priest continued matter-of-factly. "Diaz lured him here because of their resemblance to each other," he said, "and not the least in respect to their similar black beards. You see, he wanted the federal authorities to believe he himself was the one who was dead. He wanted to steal the identity of the other man, the man he strangled shortly before Jay knocked on his door."

"But this is amazing!" Jay blurted out.

Dirks, who was more used to the priest's sudden leaps and inspired guesses, pretended to take it all in stride. "At least it explains how the desk clerk and bellman were at odds over the time Diaz went up to his room," he said. "I guess they saw two different men."

"And all that business about being exactly on time," Jay said. "Timing was the key to his plan. I see that now, and I probably should have smelled something funny going on from the start. It had nothing to do with any deal."

"Well, a different kind of deal," Dirks said.

"But what was he doing?" Jay asked. "What was he doing during the twenty minutes before he came out of the bedroom in his new identity?"

"Diaz must have been in the bathroom shaving off his beard," Dirks said with a knowing smile.

"And one other thing," said Father Brown, and he wasn't smiling. "He was exchanging clothes with a corpse."

An Arrest Warrant

SHERIFF DIRKS WAS ONLY TOO HAPPY TO DO A FAVOR FOR his old friend Detective Lieutenant Henry Macdonald of the Summerfield police. The lieutenant was waiting for an arrest warrant for one Raymond Jefferson, a suspect who resided within the sheriff's jurisdiction.

Dirks prided himself on knowing virtually everyone in the county, and since he had not met this Jefferson fellow, he assumed he must be a newcomer. In any case, the lieutenant was afraid the man might slip away during the half hour it would take for the warrant to be issued, plus the time it would take him to drive over to Bardo County to make the arrest. He asked if he could fax the warrant to Dirks and then have him arrest and hold the man until someone from Summerfield could take him into custody. Dirks agreed to the plan, and after cradling the phone, he went right to work.

Macdonald had phoned early on a Saturday morning, and Dirks decided there was a good chance they would find Jefferson at home. He assigned several of his deputies to watch the suspect's residence to make sure the man did not slip away while they were waiting for the warrant. When he was satisfied his men were in position to prevent any such escape, he returned to his office and dialed the Jefferson home phone number to see if he were there. After two rings a man answered in a voice that betrayed the barest trace of a southern accent.

"Raymond Jefferson speaking."

"Mr. Jefferson," the sheriff said, taking his most businesslike tone, "this is Sheriff Dirks. In about a half hour, I'll be making a call at your home on official police business. In the meanwhile, you are not to leave the premises. I have a detail of deputies on the scene, and if you try to leave, they have orders to arrest you and detain you. Is this clear?"

"They'll arrest me?" Jefferson said. "What is this, some kind of sick joke?" He slammed the receiver down hard.

Somewhat later—it was a few minutes after the promised half hour—the sheriff arrived at the front door of the immense edifice that was the Jefferson home. It had until recently served as the residence for a successful Bardo County businessman who had retired to enjoy what pleasures the Florida sun might offer him and his wife.

Dirks pushed the doorbell button, and within a few seconds the door was opened by a middle-aged man dressed in formal eveningwear—white tie and tails.

"I'm here to see Mr. Raymond Jefferson."

"Whom should I say is calling?" The man spoke with an unmistakable British accent.

The sheriff produced his wallet and opened it to display his badge. "I'm Sheriff Dirks," he said. "And you are?"

"I am Collins. I have been in Mr. Jefferson's service for some years. He is presently at work in his study, and if you will be seated in the drawing room here on your left, I will announce your presence."

Rather than sit, Dirks thrust his hands into his pockets and stood in the drawing room's doorway where he could keep an eye on things. He thought with mild disapproval about the excessive formality of English butlers. He shrugged his shoulders. "Oh well, tally ho, and all that," he said to himself. Collins seemed to be taking an inordinate amount of time.

At last he returned, but without Jefferson in tow.

Collins bowed. "My apologies, sir," he said. "Mr. Jefferson appears to have gone out. It is most unusual. He almost always informs me in advance of his plans."

"Wait here," Dirks commanded. Then he went outdoors to interview his men. The deputies assured him that they had all sides of the house under observation and no one had left or even so much as had opened a door or window. Dirks radioed for all available deputies to report to the Jefferson home so that a systematic and thorough search might be made.

After three complete searches, with the sheriff's special emphasis on looking for hidden rooms or secret hiding places, the effort had to be abandoned. Collins had insisted throughout that he knew of no place in the house where his employer might have hidden himself. The other residents, Mrs. Jefferson and their two teen-aged daughters, professed to be no more knowledgeable of Mr. Jefferson's whereabouts than their estimable butler. Dirks, now completely out of ideas, sent his deputies off to attend to their other duties. Finally, embarrassed and ashamed, he made his apologetic phone call to Lieutenant Macdonald in Summerfield.

◼   ◼   ◼

Mrs. James led the sheriff into the parlor of the St. Dominic's rectory where they found Father Brown asleep in his favorite chair.

"Oh," Dirks said, "don't wake him. I can come back another time."

"No," Mrs. James said, shaking one of the old priest's shoulders, "he always enjoys his chats with you, Mr. Dirks, and he always seems so, well, energized after your visits."

Father Brown opened his eyes and seemed instantly wide awake and alert. "Sheriff, it's so good of you to come. Have you brought me another one of your puzzles?"

"I wish to heaven I didn't have *this* puzzle," Dirks replied. He then described everything that had happened in great detail, for he never knew which fact Father Brown might fasten upon as the key to a mystery.

When he had finished, Father Brown was silent for several minutes. At last he sighed and admitted that he could offer the sheriff no explanation for the disappearance of Mr. Raymond Jefferson.

"Well, there's some consolation in that," Dirks said. "I was afraid I had missed something obvious." He offered the priest his thanks, and bade him goodnight.

For his part, the priest went in search of the pastor of St. Dominic's, Father Bell, a man who was always a sympathetic listener. Father Brown found the much younger priest sitting in the kitchen, drinking a cup of coffee, and he joined him at the table. Then he related the story the sheriff had just told him, but he added his own interpretation and the inferences he had drawn.

"I suspect," he said in conclusion, "we will soon see a 'For Sale' sign in front of the Jefferson home."

"I'm sure you're right about that," said Father Bell.

"It really is a shame," Father Brown continued, "yet explaining to the sheriff what really happened this morning would only have made him feel more foolish than he already does."

"So, did you use the Sherlock Holmes principle that after you eliminate the impossible what remains must be the truth?"

"Partly that, but what first turned me in the right direction was the way Collins was dressed. Any Englishman will tell you that a proper butler does not wear white tie and tails in the morning. No, Jefferson used his half-hour respite to dress himself in his own evening clothes to play a part, and I would have paid good money to have heard his version of a British accent. In any event, I fear most Americans get their ideas of our English ways from the cinema or the telly."

"Blimey," said Father Bell. "Bloody hell!"

The Bathrobe

SOME YEARS AGO, CARLA JONES STARTED HER OWN HOUSE-cleaning business in the small community in which she lived. Now she was employing five women. She had designed the enterprise to serve aging retirees who could no longer keep up with their housekeeping chores, and her service was in great demand.

On the morning in question, she had an eight o'clock phone call from an Art Roberts. He lived alone, he said, and was having friends over for cocktails that evening. Could she have someone come over to tidy up? He explained that his regular housecleaner was away.

Carla usually handled these short-term and short-notice assignments herself, and so she jumped into her van and was ringing Roberts' doorbell by eight-thirty. After a few minutes, a middle-aged man with thick gray hair opened the door for her and introduced himself. Carla was surprised at his long, grubby purple bathrobe, which he held tightly closed at the neck with one hand. "I can't seem to get warm this morning," he said. "Maybe it's the flu coming on."

He asked Carla to do what she could to get the house shipshape. "And could you check right now to see that all the windows are locked and the doors bolted and chained?" he added. "I'm a bit paranoid since the burglary last summer." Carla did as he asked.

She was vacuuming industriously when, at about nine-thirty, the telephone rang. After seven rings, she decided to answer it herself. It was the office of Roberts Carpet Cleaners. "Do you know where he is?" a woman's voice asked nervously. "There are people here waiting for him." Carla promised to go upstairs and remind him.

She found him lying face down on the floor, the gray hair at the back of his head matted with blood. Carla picked up the extension. "Call the rescue squad," she said. "Mr. Roberts is unconscious, and I think he's in a bad way." Carla saw that he had discarded the purple robe and had dressed himself in a business suit. The door of the large safe next to him was hanging open. Carla felt faint. Though Art Roberts had been a total stranger to her, she could not hold back her tears.

■   ■   ■

Later in the week, Sheriff Dirks paid an early morning visit to his elderly friend Father Brown, a man he had grown to like very much, and upon whom he had learned to rely for insights when a crime had him baffled. Dirks gratefully accepted the older man's offer of coffee, and the two sat comfortably at a table in the kitchen of St. Dominic's rectory.

"The mystery is that Carla swears she bolted and chained all the doors while Roberts was still alive," Dirks began. "So how did the killer get in and out without disturbing the bolts and chains? And, look, if you're thinking it was Carla who killed him, well, no. I admit she could easily have raided the safe, and it would have taken just a few seconds for her to let herself out of the house, hide something in her van, and go back in and relock the door.

"But a violent robbery of a customer or even the scandal of being suspected of such a thing could hurt or even destroy her business," Dirks continued, ticking the point off on his index finger. "And, second, I just can't picture Carla delivering the fatal blow. The medical examiner says the killer probably used a blackjack, and it was a monster smash. It sent bone fragments into his brain."

"And third," Father Brown added, laughing and holding up three fingers, "you found nothing when you searched her van."

"Well, okay," Dirks said. "I did search her van."

"By the way," the priest asked, "what was stolen?"

"Nothing of value was left in the safe," Dirks said. "We can only assume that something was taken, but we don't know what it was."

Father Brown sat gazing at the floor, his gray eyes blinking behind his round spectacles and he seemed deep in thought. At last he said, "I don't have any firm conclusions for you, Sheriff, but I do have one notion that is consistent with the facts as you have explained them."

"Okay," Dirks said.

"I have made two guesses. My idea about the murder will not be helpful to you if either of my guesses is wrong. First, I don't think the Roberts house was burglarized last summer, and second, you did not have Carla take a close look at the corpse."

"Very good guesses," Dirks conceded. "I can't explain Roberts's bogus burglary comment, but I *can* explain why I didn't ask Carla to examine the body. She was very upset, and anyhow I had already identified the victim as Art Roberts. I knew him well. Were you going to suggest the victim was somebody else?"

"No," Father Brown replied, "but there must have been two people in the house when Carla arrived."

"Sure, that's obvious," Dirks said. "If the killer wasn't already inside, he would have found himself locked out of the house."

"We'll imagine the crime," Father Brown said. "Here are two gray-haired men together in that room with the open safe. Roberts must have opened it for some reason in the presence of the other man. Let us suppose that Roberts had something the other man wanted rather urgently, and he had possibly agreed to pay for it. We know now that he was prepared take it by force and even to kill for it. Why else would this other man have brought a blackjack with him?"

"I see that," said Dirks. "You think it was blackmail, then?"

"Perhaps it was," said Father Brown. "In any case, there was a transaction that required opening the safe. Then the other man hit Roberts with the blackjack and took something—the thing or things he had come for. He was surprised when the doorbell rang, and so he wrapped himself in that tatty bathrobe and answered the door, introducing himself as Roberts.

"Last, he sent Carla off to check the doors in other parts of the house so that he could slip out unobserved. Seconds later, Carla came back and bolted the front door, assuming that he had gone back upstairs. She did not look closely at the injured gray-haired man lying face down on the floor. She assumed it was the same man who had answered the door to let her in the house."

"Well that explains how it happened," Dirks said, "but it doesn't give any ideas about who might have done it."

"Did you find the purple bathrobe near the front entrance?" Father Brown asked.

"On the floor of the front hall closet," Dirks said. "But how does the robe figure in this?"

"I imagine it was used to cover up the killer's distinctive clothing."

"You mean a costume or a uniform? He was a postman or a soldier or something?"

"I rather think he was dressed in the worker's uniform of Roberts Carpet Cleaners," Father Brown replied. "Carla will identify him for you if he hasn't fled. If he *has* fled, then of course you'll know who he is."

Dirks took a deep breath. "I am reminded once again," he said, "of my inability to thank you properly for your unfailing help. Isn't there something I can do for you, Father?"

"Come back this evening," said Father Brown, "and we'll celebrate the conclusion of this affair by opening a bottle of Father Bell's fine claret."

Sheriff Dirks grinned. "That's a done deal," he said.

The Crime of Sheriff Dirks

ONE SUNNY MORNING IN MAY, A MAN OF VERY ORDINARY appearance known as Tiger Coffman paid a call at a dingy office building in the more downscale end of the county's commercial-industrial park. As was his frequent habit, he was visiting the place of business of his friend and associate Marty Devine. When the door had been locked and Devine had taken certain other precautionary measures, Tiger was pleased to produce two diamond necklaces for his friend's study and evaluation. After squinting at them for some minutes through a jeweler's loupe, Devine pronounced the items "pretty good stuff" and fairly easy to fence.

"I'll shop them around and let you know," he said. Tiger nodded his approval. "By the way," Devine asked, "did you see the ad in the *Register*?"

"What ad?" Tiger said with a negative shake of the head.

"You should read it. Look, I've got it right here."

The headline shouted, "$400 For Information!" Tiger sat down to study the advertisement, which continued in smaller type:

The man waiting for the shuttle across the street from A&J Jewelers and who boarded the bus at 10:45 AM Monday morning may have been witness to a crime. If you are this man and can supply a useful description of the criminal, A&J Jewelers will pay you $400 in cash, with no further questions asked. Call 955–3132.

"I'll tell you this," Tiger said. "There wasn't anyone waiting for that shuttle. This jeweler guy must have been seeing things."

"Maybe he saw you and didn't know you were the guilty party," Devine suggested. "You have to admit, not many smash and grab artists use a bus for a getaway car."

"Could be you're right," Tiger said. "I was just walking down the street when I spotted the necklaces in the window. With no one in sight and the bus coming up the street, I couldn't resist. That jeweler, old Reilly, is so slow on his feet I figured he'd never get in position to see anything useful."

Devine stowed the necklaces in a drawer, which he then locked. "So," he said, facing Tiger again, "suppose old Reilly is just fast enough to get a glimpse of somebody boarding a bus," Devine said, "and he thinks, hey, there's a witness."

"Let me use your phone, Marty."

■   ■   ■

A few days later, Sheriff Dirks dropped in on his friend Father Brown, whom he found in the parlor of St. Dominic's parish rectory reading a worn and leathery book.

"Do you have time for a cup of coffee this morning?" the priest asked.

"I thought you'd never ask," Dirks said. Father Brown nodded his head in the direction of a tea table that Mrs. James, the housekeeper, had set up with coffee mugs, teacups, and two pots. The sheriff helped himself to a cup of the coffee and a sugar-covered donut.

"To what do I owe the pleasure of your company this morning, Sheriff?" Father Brown asked, hoping for news of a puzzling crime. Now in his nineties, the old priest was no longer capable of pursuing criminals, but he had proved himself a wizard at finding answers hiding in what to Dirks seemed a meaningless jumble of evidence and testimony.

"There's not much going on at the moment," the sheriff said. "There's the usual aggravation of traffic violations. Oh, and a smash and grab, but that isn't something you would find interesting. There's no mystery in it, and I know you love mysteries as much as I dislike them."

"Tell me what was smashed and what was grabbed," the priest said.

Dirks was proud of having cracked a difficult case without the priest's help, and so he was delighted to explain how he had achieved this triumph.

"It happened at A&J Jewelers on Main Street not far from here," he said. "Last Monday a guy we know as Tiger Coffman smashed the front display window and grabbed two diamond necklaces. Old Art Reilly was in back—he's the owner—and he's not so fast on his feet any more. But still, he hobbled up to the front of the store just in time to see the thief hop on the shuttle bus across the street. Reilly gave us a description of sorts. He didn't see the man's face, but he did see enough to know the guy was of average height, average weight, brown hair, blue jeans, white tee shirt..."

"In other words," Father Brown said with a laugh, "his description might fit half the men in this county."

"It seemed hopeless," Dirks said. "We talked to the bus driver, but he didn't remember the stop or the passenger. I guess driving that shuttle gets monotonous. So anyhow, Reilly was our one witness. He says the street was deserted when it happened."

"Because the thief waited for just the right moment," Father Brown said, "or took advantage of his luck when he saw he was alone on the street with that bus coming along."

"Right," Dirks said.

"With such a hopeless start," Father Brown said, "I'm curious to know how you caught up with the thief."

Dirks grinned as he reached for a second donut. "Advertising," he said. Then he told Father Brown how he, a deputy, and the jeweler had set their trap. The afternoon after Reilly's advertisement appeared in the *Daily Sentinel*, Tiger Coffman had approached the jewelry store for the second time that week. On this occasion, unlike his earlier visit, Tiger had an appointment and he was expected.

As Dirks described the encounter, Reilly greeted Tiger with a hearty welcome. "Ah, yes indeed," he had said, "you are the very man who boarded that shuttle bus yesterday. You must have seen something."

"Sure I did," Tiger admitted. "I saw the guy who smashed your window, and if I see four hundred simoleons in real money, like the ad said, then I bet I can describe him for you." At that point, by the sheriff's account, he and his deputy appeared in the doorway leading to the shop's back room. Dirks laughed as he described how disgusted and upset Tiger had been.

"The cops," he had muttered. "I should have known you guys would stoop to a cheap trick like that. What a pack of lies! Why—why you're a disgrace to your profession."

Dirks had told his prisoner to shut up and listen. "Here's the way it falls out," he said. "You return the necklaces and pay Reilly for the broken window, and we'll plead you down to a misdemeanor."

"Law enforcement officers," Tiger had muttered, "liars, cheats, frauds, swindlers, con artists." Pressed by Dirks to make up his mind, Tiger finally gave in. "You've got your deal," he'd said.

"You mean that's the end of the story? Father Brown asked.

"Basically, yes," Dirks said. "There was nothing else to talk about. Tiger turned on his heel and stomped out through the door. So you see, Father, our advertising stunt worked just as we hoped it would."

"You let this man Tiger go free?"

"I gave him a good deal," Dirks said. "Over the years, I've gotten to know Tiger Coffman pretty well. He won't run. He may be a thief, but he's smart enough to see which side his bread is buttered on. He'll be in court when his case comes up."

"I must say," Father Brown said, "I have some sympathy for Mr. Tiger Coffman's point of view."

"What?" Dirks asked. "What do you mean?"

"I mean that a man answered an advertisement in which you promised a reward for providing a useful description of a thief. Not to put too fine a point on it, but there is no better description than producing the thief himself. I do believe in all justice that you fellows have withheld from Mr. Coffman the sum of four hundred dollars that is rightly his."

Sheriff Dirks stared at the space between his shoes for several minutes. Father Brown refused to break the silence. Finally, the sheriff said, "I'll tell the county commissioners that we incurred some miscellaneous expenses in cracking the case. And maybe I can talk Reilly into making a donation to the cause."

"Have another donut," Father Brown said, with just the faintest hint of a smile. "You mustn't let them get stale."

Dirks reached for one with white icing. "That *would* be a crime," he said.

Theory of the Case

LORAINE WAS SPEAKING TO HER DAUGHTER WITH AN urgency she hadn't used since Kathleen was a teenager. "The other day I answered the phone, and a woman's voice asked for 'Vernon Trent'. I said 'who's calling?' and she hung up on me. And yesterday your husband got a call on his cell phone, and he excused himself and went into his office to talk in private."

"Those were just phone calls, Mom," Kathleen said with a laugh. "They don't mean anything."

"They mean plenty," Loraine said. "Listen, Honey, I've been reading up on this stuff," the mother said, pointing to the cover of a newly purchased book. "A private detective wrote this: *15 Sure Signs your Husband Is Cheating.* And listen, 'Giveaway Number Three' is suspicious telephone behavior—it's all here in this book."

"I don't care *what's* in that book."

"Your husband didn't remember your anniversary. That's 'Giveaway Number Seven'. And I found this on his dresser." Loraine produced a book of matches. "What's he doing with matches if he doesn't smoke, and what's he doing with matches from the Marriott Hotel over in Groversville?"

"He must have been there on business."

"Monkey business." Loraine got up and sat down next to her daughter on the couch. "I'm sorry, Baby, but I drove over to Groversville and had lunch at that Marriott today. I wanted to see if I could find out what was so urgent that it would make your husband forget that today is his anniversary, and I wanted to know what it had to do with the Marriott Hotel. Well, I hit the jackpot. I saw Vernon there, and he was with Rita Nichols. I watched them get into an elevator, and it made me feel sick to my stomach. No, they didn't see me. But of all days, the day of your wedding anniversary! I am *so sorry*."

■　　　■　　　■

Father Brown welcomed his visitors into the parlor of St. Dominic's rectory. "May I offer you ladies some tea," he asked, "or coffee?"

"We should have made an appointment," Loraine said.

"No need for that," said Father Brown. "Please sit down and be comfortable and tell me all about—about whatever it is that has you so troubled."

Kathleen felt embarrassed, and she was reluctant to launch directly into a description of her marital problems. "We've heard rumors about you, Father Brown," she said, "—rumors that you solve all of the sheriff's problems for him. Is that true? It doesn't seem…well…"

"The sheriff solves his own problems," said Father Brown. "Still, police methods are not perfect, and when Sheriff Dirks finds himself in a cul-de-sac, he sometimes comes here to discuss things."

"What's wrong with his methods?" Loraine asked.

"When they begin an investigation," the priest explained, "the police develop what they call a 'theory of the case'. Of course, they must do this while they are still gathering facts. Usually, any new facts that surface will strengthen their theory, but sometimes the new facts don't fit, and that confuses things. I have the advantage of coming into the picture late in the investigation when all of the facts are known, and so, since I don't have a theory to defend, it is easy for me to offer a different interpretation."

"So you *start out* with all of the facts," Kathleen said. "I think I understand."

Loraine was becoming impatient. "We've got all the facts in our case," she said, "but my daughter refuses to take any action until she has your advice." And with no further preliminaries, Loraine launched into the tale of her son-in-law and his relationship with her daughter's good friend Rita.

"I have just one question," Father Brown said when Loraine had finished. "I do not know Mr. Trent. I do not think he comes to Mass with you. What sort of man is he?"

"He's a philanderer," Loraine said.

"And that's all he is?" Father Brown asked.

"He has always been considerate," Kathleen said, "unselfish, fun loving, and until now I always thought he was the most trustworthy man in the world."

"None of that means he's not cheating on his wife, Father," Loraine interjected.

"But we are merely at the stage of gathering information," Father Brown said mildly. "We will look for conclusions in due course." Then, turning back to Kathleen, he said, "You have all of your points listed there on that paper. Your points are based on that book your mother bought for you. Now add these other points—the ones you just named—'considerate'… 'fun loving', and so on. Yes, write them down. That's right. Good. Now take a moment to study *all* of the points. Then tell us if you can see any other pattern—a different pattern."

Kathleen stared at the paper. No one spoke for several minutes. At last she dropped the sheet onto the coffee table and brought her hands together with a clap. "I see it," she said.

"Good," said Father Brown. "Then let us change the subject."

"But what did she see?" Lorraine asked.

"Oh, that you will learn in due course," the priest replied. "Is that not so, Mrs. Trent?"

"Thank you for the coffee, Father," Kathleen said. "And thank you for your help. Now, Mother, we really must be going."

"But, but…" Lorraine stammered.

■   ■   ■

Vernon was home early from work that evening. That was lucky, for he had hardly enough time to hang up his coat before the phone rang.

"It's for you," Lorraine said. Her tone was decidedly icy. "It's some *woman*."

Vernon took the phone. "Hello?" he said. "Oh, hi Rita… What?…You're not kidding?…Five tickets?…Well, yeah, I'm pretty sure we're interested, short notice or not. But you better talk to Kathleen before I make it definite."

Kathleen listened for a moment. Then she said, "Absolutely! We'll start getting ready."

It was soon explained to Lorraine that Rita and her husband had tickets to a one-night-only performance by the acclaimed Elvis impersonator Ed "Hound Dog" Greene. He was playing the dinner theater at the Groversville Marriott as a stopover on his way to Chicago.

"Get ready right now," Rita had said, "because we're picking you up in half an hour."

As soon as Vernon had disappeared into the bathroom, Lorraine grabbed Kathleen by the elbow and dragged her into the kitchen.

"Listen, you little imp," she said, "I've seen that smug look on your face on a regular basis since you were four years old. Now *you* are going to tell *me* what's going on."

"Mom, your theory of the case wasn't based on all of the facts. You just used the suspicious facts, like my husband forgetting our twenty-fifth wedding anniversary and suddenly getting sneaky and taking top-secret phone calls and trekking over to the Groversville Marriott with my best friend. But Father Brown said to look at the good facts about Vern, too—that he's a thoroughly decent man."

"Good heavens," Lorraine said, the light of a new understanding dawning in her eyes. "You mean we're not going to see an Elvis Impersonator? Thank goodness."

"Mom, if you let on you know, I'll take away your television privileges for a year."

"Yes, daughter."

"And now," Kathleen commanded, "go find a mirror and practice looking surprised."

The Miser

THE NELSON BROTHERS HAD LITTLE IN COMMON. RICK was a good handyman, but he had no use for book learning. Carl was not handy with tools, but he taught math at the local high school and helped coach the football team. The one thing the two did have in common was the total absence of moral sensibility or what many would call a conscience. They were constrained from committing outrages large and small only by the fear of punishment, ridicule, or the loss of some advantage.

The two were friends as well as brothers and had grown closer after their divorces. They had been careful not to foster the bad reputations that, in reality, they richly deserved, and both men were well thought of except, of course, among their former in-laws. The two could often be seen in the Red Lion, their favorite place for plotting their secret schemes and scams.

"The man you describe," Carl was saying on one of the Lion's noisier nights, "is nothing but a loner and a miser."

"He doesn't even have a bank account," Rick said. Carl gave him a doubtful look. "No, listen, Carl, he pays me in cash, and I asked him why he never wrote a check. He said he didn't believe in them."

Carl laughed. "Believe?" he said. "Does he think banking is a religion? Anyway, a pawnbroker is a kind of banker. He gives out loans on collateral, right?"

"But see," Rick continued, "that doesn't matter because I caught a glimpse of his safe when it was open. I saw it in a mirror, and he didn't know I was watching. Look, Carl, that thing was packed with stacks and stacks of good old Grade-A folding money."

"You plan to crack the safe?" Carl said, shaking his head in disapproval.

"No, he opens the safe with a key, and he keeps the key on a cord he hangs around his neck." Carl's visible reaction to this information was a scowl that gradually turned into thoughtful contemplation. "Any ideas?" Rick asked.

"Maybe," Carl said, "but this has to be worked out with air-tight logic. We have to lure him away from the house, get the key, get the dough, and somehow not end up in striped pajamas. How much is in that safe?"

"The bills I saw were twenties, and there were, I think, about ten stacks."

"How tall were the stacks?"

"A foot tall, at least, maybe more."

Carl remained silent as if working something out. At length he said, "I'm assuming there are equal numbers of fives, tens, and twenties. So there's maybe two-hundred thousand in that safe. If it's all twenties, it could even be as much as four-hundred thousand."

After several more beers and much more conversation, Rick summed things up. "It's too good to pass up," he said.

"Don't get your fingerprints on that safe," Carl said. "Any place else doesn't matter. You're his handyman."

"Make sure nobody sees you," Rick said.

"It's private property," Carl said. "No adults are going in there during working hours and no kids will be playing there on a school day. I'll walk off every inch of the woods within a couple of hundred yards of the tree. I'll check it all out from every direction, every point of the compass. Anybody shows up and I call it off."

■   ■   ■

On the following Tuesday, Rick spent the early part of the morning at the pawnbroker's house doing odd jobs. At about ten-thirty he found his employer enjoying a cup of coffee in the kitchen.

"Say, Mr. Mills," he said, "I walked over here this morning and took a shortcut through Bailey's woods. About halfway between here and Bailey's house, there's this giant oak tree in the middle of a stand of maples, and some fool left a small metal box there on the ground half-full of gold Krugerrands."

"You didn't take them?" Mills asked.

Rick shook his head. "I'm not a thief," he said, and then, changing the subject, "I'm knocking off for the rest of the day, Mr. Mills. I have something I have to do."

Rick walked around the corner—he had parked his car where Mills wouldn't see it. He then drove to a secluded spot bordering Bailey's woods. After about a half-hour his brother walked out of the brush and handed him a key hanging on a cord.

"Smooth as silk," Carl said.

"Well, the old miser didn't waste any time getting there," Rick said.

"No surprise about that," Carl said.

Rick drove back to the pawnbroker's house. Once inside, he hurried to the safe, opened it with the key, and began stuffing stacks of bills into the two empty toolboxes he had brought with him. No one noticed him as he left the house and drove away. If any neighbors had noticed him, they would have thought nothing of it. They were used to Rick.

It took less than ten minutes for Carl to disappear into the woods with the key and jog back to the car without it. "It's around his neck and tucked into his shirt," he said. "Now let's go to my place. I told the school I was taking a sick day. I should be at home. We can stash the loot in my crawlspace."

"After we count it," Rick said. "Don't you feel guilty about cashing in on the old geezer's weakness for money?" They both laughed at this.

■   ■   ■

That evening, Sheriff Dirks found the brothers at the Red Lion. "I'm going to join you two, if you don't mind," he said.

Carl pushed back a chair. "Buy you a cocktail, Sheriff?" he said.

"Thanks," Dirks said, "but actually I'm on duty. You played hooky today, Carl?"

"Holy smokes!" Carl said. "They send out the police for that now? Well, I'm guilty as charged. Take me off to the hoosegow." Rick started to laugh at his brother's wisecrack, but he managed to suppress his giggle into something more like a grunt.

Dirks ignored him. "I was wondering if either of you happen to know how Will Mills' safe came to be empty," he said. The two brothers could think of nothing to say to this. "The thing is," Dirks continued, "we found Mills dead in Bailey's woods this afternoon. It was supposed to look like an accident—like a big limb fell from a tree and brained him."

"Well, it probably *was* an accident," Rick said.

"Here's the thing, Carl," Dirks said. "You weren't the only one playing hooky today. Bobby Bailey took the day off too. He wound up at the rectory over at St. Dominic's. He was a badly frightened youngster, and he didn't know what to do. He certainly didn't want his parents to learn he ditched school. So, he went to the one grownup he knew he could trust. I mean the old priest-in-residence there—his name is Father Brown. Old as he is, for some reason children really love the guy. Maybe it's his funny British accent."

"I don't think there is any possible way," Carl said, "for us to explain to you how little we care about your funny priests or your bratty kids."

"We have search warrants," the sheriff continued, ignoring Carl's remark. "We plan to give your places of residence a thorough going over. Like most boys, Bobby Bailey likes to climb trees, and you two know there are plenty of trees to climb in Bailey's woods. Father Brown believes you probably were convinced you looked in every direction for possible witnesses, Carl, but here's the kicker. He says you forgot that *up* is a direction, too."

Sheriff Dirks turned and nodded his head to the two deputies who had been standing inconspicuously by the wall on the other side of the room. "Now listen carefully," Dirks said to the brothers, "because I'm about to read you your rights."

Collectors

UDGE DOLE WAS ONE OF THOSE AMATEUR SCHOLARS WHOSE enthusiasm spills over into collections of relics and artifacts. His Honor's passion was American military history and, after long years of acquisition, his accumulation of weapons and documents had grown quite large and was extremely valuable. By the time he retired from the bench and bar and moved into a spacious new home in the Midwest countryside, his collections were well known and universally admired by those who shared his interests.

On the day of his violent death, the judge, long a widower, was entertaining twelve of his friends and fellow collectors. The activities began in the room Dole used as a small museum to display his own collections, which he proudly exhibited for his guests. The main entertainment of that fatal afternoon, however, was a formal slide presentation delivered by Mr. Henry Hanks of Chicago, a respected dealer in historical artifacts and an admitted fanatic on the subject the American Civil War. Hanks showed photographs of letters and dispatches from that bygone era, and these included autographed notes from Generals Grant and Lee and also an official presidential letter from Abraham Lincoln directed to Jefferson Davis.

Hank's lecture was followed by an informal cocktail reception. A catered dinner was also planned, but events intervened. Two of the guests found Judge Dole dead in his office.

The two guests had been sent by the rest of the group to call their host to dinner. No weapon was found in the office, but the medical examiner said the judge had been attacked from behind and run through the back and chest with a sword or some other weapon with a sword-like blade. At first the sheriff's police surmised that the sword in question was part of the weaponry on display in the museum; later they learned that the display cases were kept locked at all times, as were the doors and windows of that room. It was Dole's strict practice, all the guests were agreed, to hold the keys in his personal possession. Indeed, the police found the keys on a chain in his pocket.

What most frustrated the police was that the guests had been freely milling about in the victim's large home. Any of them could have slipped away from the group unnoticed to accost him.

■   ■   ■

Sheriff Dirks found himself once again at a table in the kitchen at St. Dominic's rectory, and he was even more grateful than usual when Mrs. James offered him a full stein of cold beer, for the Dole murder had not evolved into the routine investigation he had expected. His last hope lay in the remarkable deductive powers of his elderly friend, Father Brown.

"The surprise," Dirks was saying, "was that we found the sword hidden inside a hollow cane and locked in one of the museum display cases."

"According to the report in the *Sentinel*," the priest said, "it was the famous sword-cane Major Wright used against Jim Bowie in the aftermath of that celebrated duel in Louisiana."

"Yeah, well, maybe," Dirks said, "but forensics tells us it was the sword-cane used to murder Judge Dole."

"How did the judge acquire his collections?" Father Brown asked. "I'm sorry, Sheriff, but I've never been a collector myself. I don't know their ways."

"I had to look into that," Dirks said. "These people swap items of value among themselves, and of course they buy from each other and from dealers. A really valuable thing might be auctioned at a fancy place like Christie's."

"And the judge?"

"All of the above," Dirks said, "or so his friends tell us. What we have to figure out is how the sword got out of the locked case, out of the locked museum, into Dole's private office, and then back again. The testimony is that Dole did not take his weapons out of his museum. Sure, he might have made an exception, but the question is, why would he make the sword an exception when every one of his guests had already seen the thing when he showed them his collections earlier that afternoon?

"From the facts, we can only speculate that the judge brought the cane into his office so that one of his guests could examine it closely with a view to purchasing it or swapping something for it. Then we think the guest used the sword when the judge—he wasn't suspecting anything—when he turned his back to the killer. We believe this man or woman took the judge's keys, returned the cane to the museum, and replaced the keys in the judge's pocket."

Father Brown considered this. "I have no doubt that you're right," he said. "Surely something of the sort must have happened. Did any of the guests have a reason for wanting the judge dead?"

"There isn't any motive I can find," Dirks said. "Judge Dole was respected and well liked by all of his collector pals. They considered him a friend, and there isn't any hint of a love triangle or shady business dealings. We can't pin it on the caterers either. They lost a good customer.

"And to make matters even more cloudy, there doesn't seem to have been a theft. There's a written inventory list of the judge's collections, and it matches up with the items we've tallied in his museum room. Nothing was missing. All the display cases had their weapons, and the judge's five big albums of autographs were unmolested. Nobody gained anything tangible from the death insofar as we can see, and for the life of me, I can't think of any reason for murdering the judge unless it was to steal his valuables."

"And no one has suggested other lines of inquiry or theories of the case?" Father Brown asked.

"We're at a dead end," said Dirks, shaking his head. "So, Father, where do we go from here?"

Father Brown stared at table between them, a scowl on his wrinkled face, a sure signal that he was deep in thought. At length he said, "I have something you might try, Sheriff."

"What do you have in mind?" Dirks asked.

"Of course, I'm just theorizing, but I think it is reasonable to expect that some of the items in the autograph collection are counterfeits."

"What?" Dirks said. "Isn't this case complicated enough without compounding felonies? In all respect, Father Brown, I don't see how this conjecture of yours can possibly help us. It comes out of left field."

"Well, Sheriff, you might be right about that," the priest acknowledged, "but if everything is accounted for, then I think your murderer may have had false documents prepared; after the stabbing, he or she could have switched the forgeries for some of the genuine articles stored in that room. That would have the effect of concealing the theft from investigators, would it not? I believe that if you were to have an expert examine the most valuable items in those autograph albums, you would have your answer."

"Wouldn't that be a risky plan? If the thief carried away the goods, how could he be sure he wouldn't be searched?"

Father Brown waved his hands dismissively. "Letters or autographs would be small enough to be securely hidden somewhere in the judge's spacious home to be retrieved by the guilty party later—when the dust had settled, so to speak. Oh, and Sheriff, make no public announcement when you have the answer. Keep still about it."

"Well, assuming you're right," Dirks asked, "why should we keep mum?"

"You want the murderer to believe his theft has gone unnoticed. If he has the idea of selling any of the items he took, you'll have your man or woman when the item is put up for sale."

Dirks then turned the conversation to the subject of Father Brown's own collection.

"But, Sheriff," Father Brown protested, "I've already told you I'm not a collector. I have never had a collection of any kind."

"I was referring to that priceless collection of beer in your refrigerator," Dirks said.

Days later, experts studying Judge Dole's collections found a large number of hastily forged autographs, just as Father Brown had predicted. It was several months, however, before a unique set of papers with George Washington's signature surfaced as the featured item in the newly revised edition of *Collectible Antiquities*, the official catalog of Henry Hanks Associates Ltd.

Sunglasses at Night

"O RDINARILY," SHERIFF DIRKS SAID, "ANYONE TRAPPED in that sort of fire would be burned to ashes—totally cremated. But in this case, when the ceiling collapsed, the woman's body was buried in the rubble and was not completely burned up. We eventually learned from the coroner that the cause of death was a bullet lodged in her brain."

The sheriff was discussing his latest case with his two priest friends, Father Bell, the pastor of St. Dominic's, and Father Brown, an elderly priest who served as Father Bell's assistant. They were seated at the kitchen table in the parish rectory as Father Brown enjoyed his morning tea and the sheriff downed his fifth cup of coffee.

"Now we have a murder investigation starting weeks after the crime, and all the leads are cold if not completely gone."

"Yes," Father Brown said, "I see the difficulty."

"Don't get me wrong," Sheriff Dirks said, "but when I say that law enforcement is a lot easier and less complicated in a police state, I just mean that tracking someone's movements can get pretty complicated under our system—even under the best of circumstances. Cab rides are good indicators because the cabbies have to keep a log of times and addresses. Car rental records are another good source. One of the best is your head waiter. He can tell you that you had a reservation last Saturday night for seven o'clock, that you were ten minutes late, and that you left the place at eight-thirty. Anyway, it took us a lot of time with plenty of blind alleys before we got everything straight."

"So you have everything straight at last?" Father Bell asked.

"Well, I was only talking about the timing. We've got what happened and when, but not the who or the why of it."

The sheriff had just spent the better part of an hour describing the events of the evening of November 3rd. Casey Millard and his wife Janice lived together, the sheriff explained, but after Casey had retired from his career as a trial lawyer, their marriage had deteriorated to the point where they barely spoke. On most evenings, Janice stayed at home to knit and watch television while Casey went bar hopping. His habit of spending time in the apartment of Mildred Katz was an open secret.

There are not many homes in the wooded area where the Millards lived, and it wasn't until eleven o'clock on the evening in question that someone had reported that the Millard home was on fire and was rapidly becoming engulfed in flames. By the time the fire trucks reached the scene, the house had collapsed and there was little to be done but to make sure the fire did not spread. The Millards, like many householders, had a basement storage room with box after box of documents, photos, and other memorabilia, and stacks of newspapers. They also were storing two portable butane tanks, a large can of kerosene, paint supplies, and other flammables. According to Chief Hammersmith, it was a fire waiting to happen.

One of the firemen had the presence of mind to phone Mildred Katz and, after some stalling, she was persuaded to put Casey Millard on. He left immediately for his home, or what was left of it. Fortunately for him he had done what few think to do. He had rented a large safety deposit box at the bank, and that is where he kept all of his valuable papers—wills, trust documents, insurance policies, birth certificates, and the like. It was well for him, in the sheriff's opinion, that he had exercised that much foresight at least. He would have no trouble in collecting on his wife's life insurance and the insurance on the house.

"A bus ride is the most anonymous way of moving around," said Dirks. "If I walk into a bus station and buy a ticket for cash, there are no records that connect that ticket to me. And if you could chase down the passengers on a particular bus ride—which you usually can't—nobody remembers the other passengers. I mean, unless a guy dresses up like Santa Claus or something."

Father Brown considered this. "And this is why," he asked "you have no hope of identifying the man who shot Mrs. Millard?"

"That's it in a nutshell," Dirks said. "The bus arrives at nine-thirty and there's a forty-five minute layover. The passengers usually stop at the bus-station snack bar or run to a nearby restaurant if they want something fancier. But they have to be back on the bus in forty-five minutes.

"Our man found a cab outside the station and gave the driver the Millard address. The cabbie's description of him is beyond useless. Here's a guy with a trench coat, a brown trilby hat, black handlebar mustache, and—get this—he's wearing sunglasses at nine-thirty in the evening."

"Yes, I've seen that," said Father Bell, "and I've always suspected these people even wear their sunglasses to bed at night."

"Obviously, Father," the sheriff said, "this guy doesn't want to leave a useful description behind. We're assuming he wore a fake mustache. But anyhow, the cabbie takes him to the Millards and agrees to wait. He says a woman answered the door and invited Mr. Mysterious in. He says the guy was there less than ten minutes, and then he comes out, and back they go to the bus station in plenty of time for the guy to get back on his bus."

"You think he shot Mrs. Millard and set the fire to hide what he had done?" Father Bell asked.

"Yes," Dirks said, "and we also suspect that the husband might have hired this guy. But since we don't have a shred of proof, this case has to go into the unsolved file."

Father Brown folded his hands in his lap and gazed solemnly at his fingers. At length he straightened up and said, "I'm sorry your investigation did not have more success, Sheriff."

After Dirks had left, Father Brown poured himself another cup of tea and turning to Father Bell, he asked, "Do you think I should interfere?"

"You mean you can identify the stranger with the sunglasses?"

Father Brown ignored the question and said, "A man decides he wants to be rid of his wife, but he doesn't want the expense of a divorce and settlement. He removes all of his important documents from his house. Then he kills his wife by shooting her. He readies his basement storeroom for a fire, perhaps by strewing papers around and pouring kerosene on things. Next, after he has telephoned his girlfriend, he disguises himself with the mustache and sunglasses and drives himself to the bus station. The taxi driver there accepts the idea that he has just arrived by bus. The door at the man's house is answered by the girlfriend. After he leaves, she starts the fire. Then the two meet in her apartment and wait for the phone call."

"You really have a remarkable gift, Father Brown," Father Bell said, "but I know that unless an innocent person has been accused, you prefer to try to persuade the guilty party to give himself up. But look—I am quite sure Casey Millard cannot be approached in that way. And unless he did give himself up, how would they ever get a conviction?"

"The girlfriend would testify against Mr. Millard in return for a reduced prison sentence," Father Brown said.

"That seems an appropriate way for their infernal love affair to end," Father Bell said.

For a minute or so, Father Brown seemed lost in thoughts of his own. Finally he seemed to come to a decision. "I'll phone the sheriff," he said.

Very Poor Timing

WHEN SHERIFF DIRKS ANSWERED THE CALL FOR emergency assistance from two of his men—Jack Cooper and Marty Jones—he was prepared for the worst. There had been an exchange of gunfire between the two deputies and two gangsters in a motel room at the edge of town. Dirks had been told that Cooper was seriously wounded. When he arrived at the motel, he found him dead.

For some reason the two deputies had tried to surprise the gangsters rather than wait for reinforcements and a safer way to approach the situation. Deputy Jones shot one of the two—fatally as it turned out—but not before the man had put a bullet through Deputy Cooper's head.

Sheriff Dirks leaned heavily on the doorbell of St. Dominic's rectory. He was impatient and understandably distraught. Mrs. James, the friendly housekeeper, showed him into the parlor where they found Father Brown reading at a table. "Pull up a chair, Sheriff," the priest said. "I'm sure Mrs. James will be happy to bring you a glass of wine."

"No, thanks," Dirks said. "I'm actually on the job. But I'm a little upset, and I thought a chat with you might settle me down."

"Well, then," Father Brown said, "tell me what has happened."

Dirks took a seat at the table across from the priest and stared for a moment at the back of his hand. Then he said, "I lost one of my very best men, Father, and he leaves behind a wife and two young kids. It was so unnecessary. It didn't have to go down the way it did."

"*Requiéscat in pace*," Father Brown said. "I'm truly sorry, Sheriff. May he rest in peace."

"It happened like this," Dirks said. "We had a call from Art Gentry, that old white-haired guy who manages the Deluxe Motel. He told us that he rented a room to a couple of very slick and unsavory-looking mugs who drove up in a new Mercedes and were dressed in expensive-looking business suits. Gentry told us that when he walked past the window of their room he noticed a gap between the drapes, and he could see inside."

Dirks then explained that Gentry had called the sheriff's office to say that the men were sitting in their shirtsleeves and both were wearing shoulder holsters. One of the men, according to gentry, was cleaning an M-1 assault rifle. "That's not something you pick up at your local sporting goods store," Dirks said.

"You mean that it isn't a hunter's rifle?" Father Brown asked.

"It's strictly a military and law-enforcement weapon." Dirks said, and then he explained how he had radioed Cooper and Jones to tell them to check Gentry's story out, but he also had warned them not to proceed on their own. For some reason the two had decided that if they used Gentry's passkey to unlock the door to the room, the surprise of their sudden and unannounced entry would give them the advantage. The sheriff thought the plan, though a needless risk, should have worked; he wasn't sure why it hadn't. According to Deputy Jones, their entry did take the gangsters by surprise, but that didn't stop the fools from going for their guns.

"Sheriff, there is more of a mystery here than you've yet explained," Father Brown said. "I know that look of perplexity well enough to recognize it when I see it written on your face."

"You're right, Father," Dirks said, "and I was thinking just maybe you could help me think this through. The gangster we have in custody is not giving me the same story as my deputy, and I can't see what advantage he thinks he'll get out of lying about it. Deputy Jones tells a very straightforward story and it rings true. The bad guy is telling a story that doesn't make sense. I believe Jones, but what's behind this other version? Can you figure it out, Father?"

"Well, no, I can't," Father Brown said with the barest hint of a smile, "Perhaps if I knew what this other version was...."

Dirks, who had been standing, sat down at the table and explained that the gangster who survived the gun battle had told him that he thought it was the two of them against just one cop. He said that the two deputies had shown very poor timing, and his friend had shot Cooper before Jones could get inside to back him up.

"I'm not very knowledgeable about police methods," Father Brown said. "Perhaps if I knew the men involved, I might be of some help. As it is—"

Dirks left the rectory that evening a troubled man. It was not until several months had passed that he finally felt comfortable in discussing the motel shootings. When he again found Father Brown reading at the parlor table, he enthusiastically accepted the glass of Bordeaux Mrs. James offered him.

"If you remember that motel episode, Father," he said, "things have turned out way better than I expected."

"You've solved your puzzle?" Father Brown asked.

"No, I didn't mean that. I mean that Marty Jones is going to marry Jack Cooper's widow. The two children will have a father again, or at least a stepdad."

"It seems a wonderful ending," said Father Brown. "I wish I knew them. I'd like to congratulate them."

"Jones has grown up a lot since his divorce," Dirks said. "His first wife couldn't put up with his philandering ways, but I think that's past history and done with. Say, what's the matter, Father Brown? You look, well, kind of stunned."

"It's nothing," Father Brown said. "At my age, you learn to expect these sudden spells. Pray excuse me and continue your story." But as the priest seemed unusually preoccupied with thoughts of his own, Dirks decided he would not be interested in further conversation about shootings and weddings. The sheriff quickly offered him his thanks and goodnight.

When Father Brown did not return from the church by eleven that evening, the pastor, Father Bell, began to worry. To his relief, he found his friend safe in one of the pews kneeling in prayer, his knobby cane hanging from the crook of his arm. Rather than call it a night, Father Brown insisted that they sit down on the old-fashioned carpeted steps leading up to the altar and discuss something that was weighing heavily on his mind. An eavesdropper would not have been surprised to find them discussing the Old Testament.

A week later Marty Jones turned in his badge, and a very puzzled Sheriff Dirks reluctantly and sadly accepted it. The sheriff would never learn that the deputy had decided to resign from the sheriff's department only after he had suffered through a long and weighty discussion with the two Catholic priests from St. Dominic's.

Dirks would also never learn what Father Brown had deduced—that Deputy Jones had deliberately delayed his entrance into the motel room that fateful night because he had wanted Deputy Cooper's wife for himself—exactly as King David had wanted Bathsheba.

Late-Night Intruder

WE KNOW THE OLD GUY HAD A VISITOR TUESDAY NIGHT at eleven," Deputy Hansen was saying, "and that's well within the time of death as specified by forensics." Sheriff Dirks and his deputies were in the conference room of the sheriff's department, trying to make sense out of the evidence in the Maynard Litton murder case.

"Alright, then," Sheriff Dirks said wearily, "we'll go through this one more time. Just stick to the few things we know and how we know them. The son found the body…"

Deputy O'Malley cleared his throat and studied his notebook. "We know this," he said. "Gerald Litton visited his dad, Maynard Litton, last Wednesday night, at about seven o'clock. He says he visited his dad practically every night at around seven. As an only child, he says it was his habit to look in on the old duffer to check on him. The son found the father dead, and he phoned us."

"Tell me again about the time of death," the sheriff said. "That's the part I don't understand."

"Okay," Deputy Jackson said. "But if you had a videotape recorder of your own, you would see the point. They say every home will have one in a few years."

"I'm waiting for the price to come down," Dirks said. "And they also say that every home will have its own computer. What would I do with a computer if I had one?"

"My nephew has an Apple II," O'Malley said. "The computer plays chess with him."

"That's what every home needs," Dirks said.

"Here's the point," Jackson said. "The medical examiner says Maynard had been dead for twenty-four hours, give or take two-and-a-half hours. He can't be more precise because—"

"Never mind," Dirks said, waving his hand impatiently. "I'll take his word for it."

"So counting back from nine when he finished examining the body," O'Malley continued, "that puts the crime at between six-thirty and eleven-thirty the previous night, Tuesday."

"Here's where you lose me," Dirks said, and he quickly counted off three points on his fingers. "Gerald had the motive, because he's a compulsive gambler, way over his head in debt, and he inherits Maynard's money. Two, he had the opportunity, because he admits he was at the scene Tuesday from about seven to seven-thirty. Three, he had the weapon. You're telling me the old man was hit from behind with one of his own golf clubs?"

"Yeah," Jackson said, "with a putter Maynard kept there in his study."

"Opportunity, means, and motive," Dirks concluded.

"Gerald left at about seven-thirty," O'Malley said. "We know that because he went directly to the American Legion banquet, and he sat at the speakers' table in the plain sight of at least fifty people. He stayed at the Legion hall until after midnight."

The deputies had already explained to the sheriff that Maynard Litton loved "The Tonight Show with Johnny Carson," but that he usually went to bed before it started at ten thirty-five. He had programmed his videotaping system to turn the recorder on every evening to record that show.

"What happened next," Jackson said, going over the same ground again, "was that at eleven o'clock Tuesday night, somebody turned off old man Litton's videotape recorder. We know that because we played the tape, and only about twenty-five minutes of the Tuesday "Carson Show" got recorded. Then the tape switches to the last part of Monday's show, which was hosted by Joey Bishop—not Carson. But we checked the timer, and it was still set to record the whole show, all ninety minutes, Monday through Friday."

"This means," O'Malley said, "that somebody—Maynard or someone visiting him—turned off the recorder at eleven—manually. I mean, somebody must have been there to press the 'Stop' button."

"So the machine is smart enough to follow orders," Dirks said, "but what does that prove?"

"It proves that Gerald didn't do it," O'Malley said. "If it was Maynard who turned the machine off, he did it when his son was at the Legion banquet. The old geezer would have to be alive to do that, wouldn't he? Let's say, for argument, that Gerald was the killer, and Maynard was already dead at eleven. What would that mean? It would mean that somebody else got into the house, wandered into the study, saw the body on the floor, turned off the recorder, and then didn't bother to call us to report the crime. That doesn't make sense, does it?"

"At my house," Dirks said, "things have been known to turn themselves off. We call it a power outage."

"Litton's electric clocks were showing the time accurately," Jackson said. "A power failure would have caused them to stop, at least temporarily. And the utility company confirms that there wasn't any general power failure in that neighborhood."

"Let's get a fresh start on this thing tomorrow," Dirks said. In truth, he wanted to drop by St. Dominic's to see if his friend Father Brown was in the mood for a chat.

■   ■   ■

The sheriff had not been able to decide between beer or wine; as he began to recount everything he knew about the Litton case, the ever-accommodating Mrs. James served him both beverages.

"The son is our only suspect," he concluded, "but at the exact time of the murder, he was in plain view at the American Legion hall. What do you to say to that, Father Brown?"

"To that," the old priest replied, "I say you need a new suspect. What about the housekeeper," Father Brown asked, "or her husband?"

Dirks took a sip of beer. "They're neither suspects nor witnesses," he said. "Tuesdays and Wednesdays are their days off. That was our bad luck."

"Or someone else's good planning," Father Brown said.

"The only thing we know for sure," said Dirks, "is that the son didn't do it. The evidence is clear enough—except I'm not sure I can explain it to, well, to…"

"To someone as old fashioned as Father Brown?" the priest asked, with a wide grin.

"Well, let me put it this way, Father. I have seen you talking on the phone, and I've seen you listening to the radio. But I have never seen you watching TV."

"I have often thanked God for the telephone and the radio," the priest said, "but I confess I do not like watching television. It reminds me of watching tropical fish in a tank."

The sheriff laughed. Then he explained, as clearly as he could, about the elder Litton's television habits and how he programmed his recording system. "You see, Father," he said, "when our people checked the recorder's timer, they found it still held to Gerald's original instructions to record the entire *Carson Show* every night, and it was not set to a new plan that would shut it off midway through the program at eleven o'clock.

This proves there was another person with the victim at about eleven, someone who shut off the recorder, and that had to have been the murderer."

"No, Sheriff, I am sorry, you have proved no such thing," the priest said. "I was born more than ninety years ago in the nineteenth century, but even I am familiar with machines that follow orders—for example, the machine we call the alarm clock. We can, as you would say, *program* this device, which merely means we can set its timer. May I tell you a story involving such a gadget?"

"Certainly," said Dirks, who was now mightily amused.

"A man I once knew," Father Brown began, "set his alarm clock to awaken him every night at midnight so that he might welcome the new day in prayer. On a Tuesday evening, he opened his apartment's door to a visitor, *M*, who murdered him and left the dwelling before seven-thirty. The other tenants testified that on that evening they heard the sound of the alarm an hour early, because this surprised them after years of hearing it ring at midnight. *M* returned the following evening, Wednesday, at seven, and finding the alarm-clock owner dead, of course, he summoned the police. They concluded that an intruder killed the victim at about eleven the previous night, because someone had caused the alarm clock to ring at that time—the wrong time—even though it was now plain that the clock was still set to ring at midnight, as always."

"But that is not anything like the same, Father," Dirks protested. "In your story, the visitor could have set the alarm to ring at eleven to make it seem like there was an intruder. Then, when he returned the following night to discover the body, he could have set the clock back to ring at midnight and then called the police."

"Yes," said Father Brown, "and your Gerald Litton could have done precisely the same thing with the recording device that was attached to his father's telly."

Dirks considered this, began to say something, thought better of it, and then he calmly poured the contents of his wine glass into his half-full beer stein.

Father Bell, who had just entered the room, said, laughing, "Why, Sheriff, I see you've invented a new kind of thirst-quencher."

Father Brown smiled, but he did not laugh.

The Busybody Club

THE SHERIFF WANTED TOMMY MOSS ARRESTED. THE youngster had been accused of grand theft by five of the town's leading citizens, and they wanted Tommy's hide nailed to the jailhouse door. But old Bill was a rare kind of sheriff's deputy. He prided himself on the arrests he did *not* make.

If Bill could talk sense to a youngster, scare him a little, and maybe assign him some chores, it seemed much better to Bill than arraignment, a criminal record, and possible detention in a juvenile facility. Keeping the peace in a small town is partly diplomacy, isn't it? At least those were the arguments Bill used with Sheriff Dirks.

Tommy worked after school at the Royal Hotel as a porter. There was a regular Tuesday night poker game in one of the rooms, which, of course, was illegal. But the prominence and influence of the players—the mayor, a doctor, the president of the bank, and two lawyers—was such that Sheriff Dirks chose discretion rather than a narrow and pedantic interpretation of the statutes. Lesser townsfolk referred to the five players simply as "the Busybody Club," but that name was never uttered in the presence of any of the worthy members of that fraternity.

On every Tuesday night, each of these gentlemen pitched two hundred dollars into a tin box and took a stack of poker chips. At the end of the evening they traded their chips back for the cash. At the end of the previous evening, however, they had found the tin box empty. Tommy was accused, roughly searched, and then marched down to police headquarters. The search had not turned up the missing money. Bill refused to arrest the lad.

"Just let me talk to them, Sheriff," Bill begged, "tonight, at the hotel."

"It might be a good idea," Dirks conceded. "Get them off my back and onto yours."

That evening, the elderly deputy met the members of the Busybody Club at the table in the room where the five played poker on Tuesday nights. "I asked you here," he began, "because I want to demonstrate something, and unless you see it with your own eyes, you won't believe me."

"Just get on with it," the mayor said.

Bill put his small two-way radio on the table and then showed them a playing card—the ace of hearts. He held it up in the air and said, "What's the card, Jack?"

The radio crackled, and a voice said "Ace of hearts." Bill had the mayor pick a card and hold it up. "Three of clubs," the radio said.

"Did you know," Bill asked, "that there's a good view through this window from the roof across the street? Jack's over there now. Look, you can see him. And he can see us."

"So what?" the mayor said, but for the first time that evening Bill had the full attention of all five members of the Busybody Club.

"There's a lot to see looking through hotel windows," Bill said. "A kid standing on that roof over there might see something he isn't meant to see.

"I know a kid who was watching this room last night. I'm not saying who, because he's got a papa who's too quick to reach for the razor strap, and I don't think this boy deserves a beating. The boy and I have an understanding, and I'm going to be watching him."

"What did the kid see?" the doctor asked.

"Well, I'll stick to just one thing he saw. He saw someone take money out of your tin box."

"There wasn't anybody here to take it but Tommy," one of the lawyers said.

"Tommy and five men," Bill said, and before anyone could protest, he added, "Listen. I know why you blamed Tommy. No, hear me out. None of you lacks for money, and so you think that none of you has any reason to steal. But I know that people steal for lots of reasons other than need. So, here's the plan, gents. Tomorrow, one of you will put a thousand dollars into a plain envelope with the sheriff's name on it, and put it where he'll find it. Front seat of his car, maybe. Then we'll just forget the whole thing." "There isn't going to be any envelope," the mayor said.

"Fine," Bill said. "If there's no envelope, I'll just have to send my young witness to the State's Attorney."

　　　　■　　　　　　■　　　　　　■

Sheriff Dirks decided he had a real problem, and the problem was not an unsolved crime. The problem was Deputy Bill. Dirks dropped in on his friend Father Brown, and carefully recounted the conversation between Deputy Bill and the Busybodies.

"I don't condone the use of threats, Father Brown."

"Your deputy's remarks to those four gentlemen struck me rather as a bluff than a threat. But pray continue, Sheriff."

"I can't imagine how you jumped to the conclusion that it was a bluff, Father, even though, as it turned out, it *was* a bluff. Well, anyway, the next day I found an envelope with one thousand dollars in the front seat of my car. I passed the envelope to the mayor, and so the Busybodies dropped the charges against Tommy. I congratulated Bill, and then I asked him to tell me which of the Busybodies took the money."

"And he told you that Tommy took it," Father Brown said.

"How on earth did you figure that out?"

"And Tommy returned the money?"

"That's right, Father," Dirks said. "Bill defended what he had done by accusing the Busybodies of trying to ruin the lad's life. In his opinion those men are nothing but self-righteous hypocrites. That's what he called them, and that was how he tried to excuse all those lies he told. There wasn't any kid peeping at them from that roof. He just made all it up. A pack of lies."

Father Brown gazed at the floor between them, a deep frown wrinkling his face. The sheriff had learned not to interrupt these meditations.

At length, the old priest sighed and clapped his hands on his knees. "Sheriff," he said, "what Bill told those men was strictly true. He told them that it is possible to see into the hotel from the nearby roof. Then he said a lad had been watching the room and had seen someone take the money. You see, Tommy *was* watching the room and he *did* see someone take the money— himself. Your men deceived *themselves* when they improperly connected these two truths."

"That's all well and good, Father," Nick said. "So maybe technically Bill didn't exactly tell lies to those five men. But what he *did* do in that hotel room was nothing but a scam. The way he left things, those men now suspect each other of being thieves. Their poker club has fallen apart in suspicion and distrust."

"If they have such poor opinions of one another," said Father Brown, "they are only sharing the consensus of their neighbors, or so you have told me. People call them 'the Busybodies'? Perhaps it is well that they will no longer associate with one another in a club."

"There's been a grave injustice, Father!"

"Not really, Sheriff," the priest replied. "Explain to me why Bill called them 'hypocrites'? It is not a good thing to be a busybody, and it is not really admirable to demand revenge on a mere boy. But these things, whatever else they are, are not *hypocritical*."

"Well, then," Dirks replied, "what do you make out of the word?"

"Bill has been a sheriff's deputy for many, many years," Father Brown replied. "I doubt that it is only *today's* juvenile delinquents he's refused to arrest."

"I see," Sheriff Dirks said, looking ruefully at his friend. "*Now* I see."

The Life of the Party

EDGAR "DOC" SMALL AND HIS WIFE JANIE WOULD HAVE been considered a power couple if there had been such a concept in their small hometown. Janie was pretty and vivacious, and Doc was the life of every party. He had the reputation, as his friends jokingly put it, for being "the host with the most." It was Doc who talked everyone into making fools of themselves over a game of charades, or belting out songs with the help of a karaoke synthesizer, or joining an amateurish staging of *Guys and Dolls*, or learning to sashay to the musical instructions of a genuine square-dance caller.

He was full of such ideas, and he had the enthusiasm to go along with them. He never seemed to have any trouble convincing his friends to join these silly enterprises; in retrospect, they always said it had been marvelous fun.

Doc's lifelong friend Gus Green was doing modestly well in life. He was a pharmacist who had eventually opened his own drugstore. Doc Small had done considerably better as a physician and general practitioner. The only thing unusual in the relationship between the two was that Gus, the druggist, hated Doc, the physician. He hated him with a deep and undying hatred.

It was envy. Doc was smarter than Gus, more successful, and more entertaining, but the crowning blow had to do with Janie, the love of Gus's life. She had refused Gus when he proposed marriage to her, choosing to marry Doc instead. Gus would have murdered Doc years ago if he had any notion of how to get away with it.

Doc was so used to popularity he had not an inkling of how Gus really felt about him. He simply assumed Gus was just another pal. That was why he invited Gus over to help plan the next bit of foolishness for a Saturday night party. The two began their discussion over manhattans mixed up in Doc's well-appointed party room—which featured its own bar, a small but serviceable dance floor, and a raised platform for theatricals.

"Nobody can know about this but you and me, Gus," Doc said. "I'm not even telling Janie."

"You're the host," Gus conceded. "What's it all about?"

"I'm going to stage one of those murder-mystery-for-fun things," Edgar said, "but I'm not hiring professional actors or buying one of those murder-mystery kits. This is going to be strictly do-it-yourself."

"How does it work?" Gus asked.

"It's simple," Doc said. "At about nine, when everybody's in the party room and accounted for, I'll excuse myself and go upstairs. Privately you'll have told Charlie about the game, and that I'm the victim and he's the murderer. Tell him he's to slip out so nobody will notice, and he's to wait in the wine cellar. After the murder, everybody will question everybody else, but tell Charlie he's the only one permitted to tell lies. He'll play along—Charlie's a quick study—but I don't want him to have time to think up any ideas of his own, so don't warn him ahead of time before the party starts.

"When I see Charlie go through the cellar door, I'll count to twenty and then I'll scream like holy hell. I'm being attacked and murdered and so on. You'll be in position by the stairs, and you'll tell everybody to sit still and then you'll come up for a look. I'll be lying there with a rope around my neck, a BB gun on the floor, and a suspicious looking bottle in my hand. You'll tie my hands and feet—and be quick about it, this doesn't require good knots or anything. Then you'll tell everybody to come up to the bedroom where you'll explain to everyone that I've been murdered. We'll all adjourn to the party room to see if the group can figure out who dun it."

"So the idea is that people aren't sharp enough to remember who was in the living room when you shouted out?" Gus asked.

"They will gradually piece it together, after a funny interval of confusion and contradiction," Doc replied. "People don't remember a negative—I mean they can't recall what they didn't see. They'll talk about who they were standing next to, or who they were chatting with or watching, and sooner or later they'll put the finger on Charlie by the process of elimination."

Gus, as always, agreed to help. There began to form in the back of his mind a horrible, grisly idea; the more he thought about it, the better he liked it. He was a pharmacist, and pharmacists have resources.

On that Saturday night, a happy bunch of partygoers found their way to Janie and Doc's house. Doc's usual guest mixture was on display—atheists and believers, youth and age, old friends and new faces.

Shortly after nine, Doc excused himself and went upstairs. Gus took Charlie aside, but he did not mention the murder-for-fun game as he had promised. Instead, Gus said that their host wanted Charlie, who knew all about wines, to bring a few more bottles up from the wine cellar. Charlie readily agreed and disappeared down the cellar stairs. About twenty seconds later, and right on schedule, there was a horrible scream from above. "Help! Help!" a man's voice wailed. "I'm being murdered! Help me! Murder!"

Some of the guests looked shocked and frightened. Others giggled. Janie rolled her eyes. "Now what?" she muttered.

Gus, who was standing near the stairs, told everyone to stay put. Then he ran up to the bedroom where Doc had just finished laying out his props.

"Wind the rope around my ankles, Gus," he said. "Then go get the gang." When Gus bent over with the rope, Doc felt the tiniest of pinpricks in his right ankle. Gus waited a few seconds and then put the murder-mystery props in the closet. Then he went quickly down the stairs.

"Somebody phone for the sheriff and the rescue squad," he said. "This is not a party stunt. Something terrible has happened." What happened, he thought, was that fast-acting poison had been introduced into the blood stream of their host, and two dozen partygoers would swear he, Gus, was with them in plain view at the time of the attack.

Gus looked over the group with great satisfaction. I'm in the clear, he said to himself. What a great bunch of rubes they are. The Smiths haven't a full brain between them, and Joe and Molly Burns are as dull as cattle. I have nothing to fear from that stupid beanpole of a sheriff when he shows up—that's for sure.

And most laughable of all is this ancient relic of a superstitious Catholic priest who shouldn't be allowed to roam free without a keeper. Why would Doc invite somebody like him? Look at him, Gus thought with satisfaction; look at him gazing at me with the dull, stupid eyes of an ox. What was his name? Oh, yes, Brown. I really wish he'd stare at somebody else for a while. He's starting to give me the creeps.

TAN·BOOKS

TAN Books is the Publisher You Can Trust With Your Faith.

TAN Books was founded in 1967 to preserve the spiritual, intellectual, and liturgical traditions of the Catholic Church. At a critical moment in history TAN kept alive the great classics of the Faith and drew many to the Church. In 2008 TAN was acquired by Saint Benedict Press. Today TAN continues to teach and defend the Faith to a new generation of readers.

TAN publishes more than 600 booklets, Bibles, and books. Popular subject areas include theology and doctrine, prayer and the supernatural, history, biography, and the lives of the saints. TAN's line of educational and homeschooling resources is featured at TANHomeschool.com.

TAN publishes under several imprints, including TAN, Neumann Press, ACS Books, and the Confraternity of the Precious Blood. Sister imprints include Saint Benedict Press, Catholic Courses, and Catholic Scripture Study International.

**For more information about TAN,
or to request a free catalog, visit
TANBooks.com**

**Or call us toll-free at
(800) 437-5876**

TAN·CLASSICS

A collection of the finest literature in the Catholic tradition.

978-0-89555-227-3

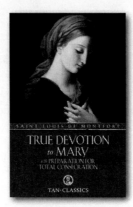

978-0-89555-154-2

978-0-89555-155-9

Our TAN Classics collection is a well-balanced sampling of the finest literature in the Catholic tradition.

978-0-89555-230-3

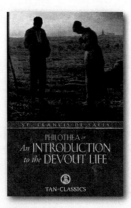

978-0-89555-228-0

978-0-89555-151-1

978-0-89555-153-5

978-0-89555-149-8

978-0-89555-199-3

The collection includes distinguished spiritual works of the saints, philosophical treatises and famous biographies.

978-0-89555-226-6

978-0-89555-152-8

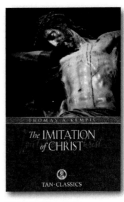

978-0-89555-225-9

Visit us at TANBooks.com

Spread the Faith with . . .

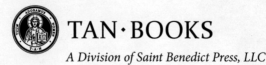

TAN·BOOKS

A Division of Saint Benedict Press, LLC

TAN books are powerful tools for evangelization. They lift the mind to God and change lives. Millions of readers have found in TAN books and booklets an effective way to teach and defend the Faith, soften hearts, and grow in prayer and holiness of life.

Throughout history the faithful have distributed Catholic literature and sacramentals to save souls. St. Francis de Sales passed out his own pamphlets to win back those who had abandoned the Faith. Countless others have distributed the Miraculous Medal to prompt conversions and inspire deeper devotion to God. Our customers use TAN books in that same spirit.

If you have been helped by this or another TAN title, share it with others. Become a TAN Missionary and share our life changing books and booklets with your family, friends and community. We'll help by providing special discounts for books and booklets purchased in quantity for purposes of evangelization. Write or call us for additional details.

TAN Books
Attn: TAN Missionaries Department
PO Box 410487
Charlotte, NC 28241

Toll-free (800) 437-5876
missionaries@TANBooks.com